I0727603

THE PENTAGON TAPES

What the Pentagon's CCTV cameras saw on 9/11

Kerry Cox

Copyright © 2022 (Kerry Cox)
All rights reserved worldwide.

No part of this publication may be reproduced or transmitted in any form or by any means, electronic or mechanical, including photocopy, recording, or any information storage and retrieval system, without permission in writing from the author.

Author: Kerry Cox
Title: The Pentagon Tapes
Genre: Fiction
ISBN: 978-1-922920-05-8

Disclaimer

This is a work of fiction. Although its form is that of an autobiography, it is not one. Space and time have been rearranged to suit the convenience of the book, and with the exception of public figures, any resemblance to persons living or dead is coincidental. The opinions expressed are those of the characters and should not be confused with the authors.

About the Author

iii

Born in Brisbane 75 years ago, finishing school 1963 for a stint in the Army after which he happily joined the ranks of the many in the hospitality industry before the events of Sep 11 2001 changed the whole world.

The reason I have written this book is because of the lack of disclosure by the relative authorities of images recorded at the Pentagon on that day other than the one image that is supposed to show an 'aircraft' crashing into the building, and after that. there was Nothing.

And I wondered why this could be and came up with all the reasons why those questions could make interesting book.

Chapter 1

VALUES

The first draft of what was to become the Constitution of the United States of America was tabled in Congress in 1786 for the vote of acceptance, but amendments were suggested that resulted in the final draft being presented some 10 months later in 1788 by its author, James Madison.

On that day, the amended draft was unanimously accepted by all those present, the document becoming the guiding light that all Americans from that day forward have built their nation and character on.

Since that historic day, all Americans, every day, from all walks of life swear the oath of allegiance to the United States and its Constitution, to forever uphold all that it stands for.

These people are called patriots, no matter who or from what walk of life they come.

Those who swear the oath each day are declaring that they would defend and hold sacred what all Americans stand for and believe in because of what it says is truth.

Most people take for granted that all the duly elected political leaders, representatives, and diplomats will act on their behalf to defeat all that threatens the very existence of the nation of free men, and with deadly force if need be.

The United States of America has also made an offer to the rest of the world that it will come to their aid to defeat tyranny and oppression, wherever these evils raise their ugly heads.

But every once in a while, there have been some who thought that their actions in government were done with the nation in mind and with the best of intentions, only to find that their judgement was deemed to be poor, and sometimes treasonous. Indeed, some have even paid the ultimate price for this.

There have been times in America's history when a true patriot steps forward when an injustice is seen to be done and does something about correcting that injustice, no matter the personal sufferings endured in the pursuit of that quest.

On August 23, 1996, a young man named Bevan Johansen Kleindinst graduated top of his class from Cal Tech at the age of 24, with a degree in computer science and engineering.

On December 1, 1996, he married his childhood sweetheart Phillipa Alice Wilson. Almost one year later, he joined the United States Air Force on September 15, 1997.

After his Air Force boot camp training, he was posted at the Milden Hall Air Base in England on January 1998, where he served for two years as flight crew on board the electronic eavesdropping aircraft that flew across the European continent on "snooper" missions.

Thanks to his dedication and efficiency, he was duly promoted to the rank of lieutenant within the first 12 months of his posting there.

The end of his tour of duty in Europe saw him transferred back to the USA in October 2000, where he would serve the final years of his time in the Air Force as manager of computer security, overseeing the new mainframe computer system for data storage that had just been installed at the Pentagon.

He liked to think that his posting at the Pentagon came about as a result of his earlier transfer applications outlining his knowledge and hands-on problem solving, and mainly because of his expertise and extensive knowledge of mainframe computer systems security and programming.

The fact is that he had top secret security clearance was, for him, pending his eventual discharge from the Air Force, a logical posting.

And being the senior systems analyst at the Pentagon, he knew it would help him maintain and update his skills in preparation for his return to the open market of free enterprise and the rewards to be had by working with the most advanced companies that were developing faster computer systems for both civil and US military applications.

Thinking long term, he was planning that at the end of his military service, he would take up Honeywell Systems' offer to him.

He had worked for them before he joined the Air Force and they had been constantly reminding him to rejoin the firm upon his discharge.

He also knew that to return to the research and development department of Honeywell at their San Jose facility in California would be a smooth transition, especially with his skills and expert knowledge of computer sciences; indeed, for him, it would be the perfect end to the choices he had made that let him achieve, in his way, to live the American dream, to be a success on all levels.

Chapter 2

ORIENTATION

The day he presented himself for duty at the Pentagon was the day he became fully aware of the enormity of his assignment.

When Bevan first took up his post at the Pentagon, he attended his induction orientation, where he saw in his brief just how extensive the security system of the Pentagon complex was.

Every office and room in the Pentagon, from the directors of all departments to the janitors rooms and bathrooms, were all under constant closed circuit video and audio surveillance, 24/7.

But most excitingly, he would be assigned to oversee the department where the mainframe computer he was to work with was housed deep in the bomb-proof bunker-style basement.

As the officer in charge and as the senior computer systems analyst, his first priority was to screen every member of his department to make sure everything was up to speed.

He was now able to recruit the best people he could find that had previous experience in analysing computer data, beginning with key people from within the Air Force intelligence community, people that he could rely on to be vigilant in all they were asked to do.

This was supremely important as the nation's sense of security come from those who hold the front line and tell us everything is OK.

His attention to detail was to prove vital in the first twelve months of taking up his assignment. His work ethic was to again see him promoted further up the chain, promoted to the rank of captain. In August 2001, he was promoted to major, after being assigned the staff he had asked for who he then personally trained to operate and maintain the most recent IT system, one that he had originally helped design and implement, all in conjunction with the Honeywell Systems engineers he had previously worked with.

Installed in the late 1980s, the system was programmed in such a way that at a specific time each day, all the recorded video images and audio from the internal security system was automatically downloaded to the mainframe computer where it was stored, to await "classification" prior to being stored in the National Library in Washington DC.

And now, after the most recent upgrade, each individual item recorded during the day was now automatically burned onto high-capacity digital storage disks, which would then await classification before it was either destroyed or determined to be for the final storage destination at the US Congressional Digital Library.

It was while he was at the Pentagon that he helped design and implement a 'lossless' digital storage programme created for the transfer of long-term storage of all the older analogue video/audio system, making it possible to overcome the 'degradation' associated with the early VHS format.

It was a problem that had plagued the analogue system, preventing the long-term storage and duplication of these VHS video recordings.

The degradation was caused mainly by background electrical energy fields that alter the magnetic tapes and distort the data with no recovery possible.

That was until Bevan's digital revolution discoveries and the benefits in their application, including all the phone and fax communications that previously came in and went out of the Pentagon on a daily basis.

As a computer programmer, Bevan had always looked at making the workload on the CPU less complicated.

The programme he had designed made it possible for an operator to screen and classify the data more quickly, making it ready for transfer to the US Congressional Digital Library in a fraction of the time it had previously taken to get it where it could be seen and heard with the same clarity as the moment it was first recorded, for all time.

The original mainframe that was installed in the Pentagon was made by IBM and the operating system "language" at the time was COBOL.

It was an analogue system originally designed for all video and audio mass storage, before the digital format that is in use today forced a change to the way data was processed.

Prior to his taking up his post at the Pentagon, all the data gathered by the system was originally stored on extremely large reels of magnetic tape of only 10,000 megabytes (10 Gigabytes) each.

With the recent upgrade replacing the analogue tape system, the 'solid state' digital storage system now holds all the gathered data on five hard drives of 300 Gb each, being held for three months, during which time it was screened and then classified, and subsequently transferred to the United States Congressional Digital Library archive for permanent storage for 15 years.

The bulk of this data was compiled from the 'in house' IBM recording and surveillance system that was, at that time, the most secure computer system in America.

But now, it had outgrown its premises and was due for a total transfer to macro digital for permanent and safe storage for all to see...eventually.

In January 2000, the biggest ever upgrade of the computer system was initiated after the computer system Bevan was about to inherit had been hacked just before he was assigned.

The culprit was a young hacker from Culver City, causing a great deal of anxiety within all government agencies, especially within the Department of Defence, the FBI and the CIA. As a result of the security breach, his assignment was, after his programme upgrade, to prepare a new programme that was to be implemented and used by all future operators of the programme that was able to detect and prevent any future external 'hack attack.'

Bevan was also involved in developing a training syllabus for all new staff of the processes that would help classify all this material more easily, on one central computer mainframe.

Having the highest level of security clearance, his sole responsibility was to make sure that all the video and audio recordings that had been gathered on these computer systems were screened, classified, and archived on the most secure computer in the world.

It was a huge responsibility.

So much data was recorded and stored on the new system in such a short time, that it might present a security risk and It became imperative that all this information should be processed into a compressible digital format as soon as possible.

Bevan had only been on the job at the Pentagon for 12 months when it was decided that the upgrade was to happen.

He was quite at home with the system he had created and operated and was often amused by some of the antics the staff got up to, especially of those who forgot that they were being recorded.

Such recordings, classified as 'of no importance' (ONI), were among those that never made it to the CDL and were deleted from the system, but they made funny conversations at his home gatherings whenever he had some of his new friends (most of them ex-Air Force) from the Pentagon Computer Department over for a cookout.

It was a bright Tuesday morning, just like every other day, but he arrived a little bit early and had time for a quick coffee in the canteen, chatting and catching up with some of the officers he had become friendly with since his posting.

But this particular Tuesday was to be indelibly marked in his brain for the rest of his life.

It was September 11th, 2001.

At 9:32 AM, all hell broke loose. Just as he was loading up the first of the disks to be classified, he felt the whole building shake, like it was an earth tremor, or so he thought.

But within seconds of feeling the building shaking, alarms sounded and over the internal public address system came the order to evacuate the building.

As with previous evacuation drills, he initially did not take it seriously. But as he ran along the highly polished corridor to the emergency exit, the smell of cordite and dust quickly changed his mind.

Had a bomb gone off? Or a gas leak? He just didn't know!

When he reached the lawn area outside the Pentagon building, everything was in chaos.

There were people running in all directions in a panic, with sirens wailing all over the place.

Fire trucks were rushing to where black smoke was billowing into the air on the other side of the complex.

His concerns soon grew into a state of self preservation and, for the first time in his life, he felt fear.

Little did he know right there and then, that it was the day that the whole American way of life did a total U-turn.

As news of all these events filtered through via phone, TV, radio, and the internet, it was fast becoming obvious from all reports that the security of the Pentagon had been compromised in an apparent terrorist attack.

It was being reported that an aircraft had been deliberately crashed into the east side of the Pentagon, crashing at very high speed into what was supposedly the most secure complex in the world.

Moreover, two other airliners also had been flown to strike into the two World Trade Centre buildings in downtown New York City. America was suddenly, according to the media, "under terrorist attack."

The nation "on her knees."

The Pentagon was immediately put into "lock down," at the orders of the Défence Secretary Donald Ruskin, and only security staff were permitted to access the facility until a better understanding of what had happened was investigated.

It was the longest couple of days in his life, as he was totally in the dark about everything that had happened, just like the rest of America and the free world, with every American glued to their TVs in shock and disbelief at what was being rapidly being promoted by government agencies as an "An attack on our democracy".

Over the next couple of days, he was hearing on the news reports that the CIA had taken all CCTV tapes from all the venues that had surveilence video cameras in place around the Pentagon, saying they wanted to analyse them to ascertain exactly what had happened.

The following couple of days were confusing, as Bevan had been watching the endless stream of visuals of the twin towers collapsing and hearing all the reports from the top US investigation agencies about who they suspected had done this despicable thing to the American people.

America was "under attack" by terrorists according to President Bush and all members of the US government.

Time had almost stood still for the following month, as all that was on TV was the aftermath and live images of the destruction of the World Trade Centre, which was soon turned into being called "Ground Zero" by President Bush and the mainstream media.

It was at an in-house security brief when he had heard some of the staff talking about a conspiracy nut who had made a video documentary which alleged that "9/11 was an inside job."

Having always been a curious and analytical person, he began to wonder what the video contained and why it was causing so much controversy, even within the ranks of the normally conservative members of the Pentagon staff.

If there was any possibility that there could be some substance to what he had heard, he had to make an analytical assessment of his own; after all, that was what he was and what he was trained to do.

He had been trained to be suspicious about all forms of communication and its content and possible hidden meaning.

However, before he went down that road, he had to make sure that he was well covered in his acquisition of this video, 'Loose Change.'

He was very aware that others had lost their jobs for accessing websites 'of the enemy.' and he didn't want to meet the same fate.

After downloading the video from the internet, Bevan watched 'Loose Change' time and time again, gradually understanding the intent of the documentary makers efforts to sow seeds of doubt in the viewers mind that what we saw was not all it was being made out to be.

It greatly alarmed him to see what was on this video, especially as there was a great deal of logical statements that raised questions and provided some possible answers posed by its makers of what happened and why.

One of the nagging questions included in the documentary was the reference to the limited amount of damage to the part of Pentagon where the aircraft reportedly impacted, something which he had also seen first-hand and in his mind, he agreed that there should have been a lot more damage than there actually was is a commercial aircraft carrying passengers.

In fact, he had been wondering about that from the first moment he saw the big hole in the side of the building, and if it was true that a full-sized commercial passenger aircraft did hit the Pentagon complex, surely the damage would have been more catastrophic and extensive?

He remembered that day when he made it to where all the commotion had been happening and saw the big round hole in the outer wall and intense fires there. He saw first-hand the exterior of the building where the aircraft had supposedly smashed into.

He found it strange that there was not more damage than there was and the smell of cordite didn't fit the story of a plane full of jet fuel crashing into this building.

The events of that day were to affect Americans from all walks of life, both directly and indirectly, for many years to come.

For Bevan, however, it could not have been more personal, knowing that his brother in the very aircraft that was supposed to have hit the Pentagon.

It became very important to him personally to look more objectively at all these recent events through different eyes—the eyes of a highly trained analyst, not as someone who had just lost a loved one in that tragic crash.

Here he was, at the crossroads of his life, now fully aware of the fact that there must be this information available, other than just the couple of blurred images of an explosive event at the Pentagon that had been released by the US government from the CCTV camera that was located in the car park of the Pentagon .

But knowing how extensive and comprehensive the video surveillance system at the Pentagon was, he became convinced that the impact of the aircraft hitting the building would have to have been recorded by some of the CCTV cameras somewhere in the building, including the cameras that were destroyed in the impact zone and either side of the damaged area.

He started thinking of how he could start sourcing this information without raising any unwanted attention from anyone as he conducted his search.

The possibility that there was any visual and audio record from the Pentagon's extensive internal and external surveillance system was very real and he knew and was thankful that it was something that the CIA and FBI would never have any unwarranted access to.

Not as long as he still held the "keys."

This fact played heavily on his mind, and anything that existed of the events that happened on that fatal day, he knew it would have to eventually end up on a disk in his computer system, and automatically be downloaded to the central mainframe from the Pentagon's inside cameras—and all he had to do, was find it!

As he had only ever seen government-released video footage on TV and had assured everyone that it was indeed the actual impact of the aircraft hitting the side of the Pentagon on 9/11, plus what he saw in the 911 documentary, "Loose Change," the footage touted by the media and government did not convince him it was real.

And now, his nagging uneasy feelings helped him decide that he had a duty to his dead brother and all the others who died on that day, that he must find this evidence so that the whole matter presented by the "Loose Change" theory could be debunked and the issue finally put to rest.

As opposed to what was presented in the documentary "Loose Change," it was hard to disbelieve, let alone question, what the government had been saying about the tragic events of 9/11 being a terrorist attack because, every day, he was hearing nothing but that, and because he believed that the President was not being untruthful with America about the event.

It was against all that he had been taught as a young man, that we all lived with a system of government that guaranteed liberty and justice for all, a nation with values the whole world admires, represented by a President the whole world loves. But it was becoming evident that no one liked what Bush had done or the road he was leading the nation down.

If there was anything to confirm what had been alleged in "Loose Change," he knew it was to be found on a disk in a Pentagon computer; he now felt sure it existed.

As there were plenty of other disks he had seen so far that came from everywhere else inside the Pentagon on that day, except from that particular area, and he had seen thousands of disks over the last year that convinced him that it was possible it could be found, so, he decided to look for all visual and audio recordings of the event with that date and time stamp that he now believes could and should exist.

He was getting more and more relieved to know that since the event, there had been no request that he was aware of, by anyone or any agency, to obtain what was obviously stored on the central computer of the actual event!

Why no requests for such vital information?

The Department of Internal Security, which he had headed for the last year, has always been housed in the basement area of the Pentagon. It was only accessible to those who had security clearance for that area who could access that particular computer, except for those who worked in the United States Congressional Digital Library.

However, the people assigned there had only one interest, and that was to put what was given to them "on the shelves" and go home, so anyone from the outside who would have tried to gain access to this area or the data stored there would have found it impossible to do.

In the aftermath of the security breach involving the Pentagon's computer network, all US government departments, especially the Department of Defence, instigated a permanent lock down to make sure there would be plenty of warning that the system was under attack.

Designed to prevent any more unauthorized releases of any data that may be of some embarrassment to the US government and, because of this vigilance, the data stored now that had to be screened was now designated a certain 'value.'

As he personally assigned this 'value,' he was the only one who decided which material was to be retained for archiving in the

USCL and materials that were not, according to his classification, of a 'sensitive nature,' were destroyed.

The new programme he designed enabled him to expedite the process of classification, starting with each 'pack' being allocated a file number, a date and time tag that were etched onto the physical face of the disk. Data that was on that disk was then burned onto a high-capacity DVD, which was then physically stored in a secure pre-classification filing system, similar in many ways to the type of storage facility that was used for the paper records system it initially replaced.

Every item that was sent to the classification department also had its own unique location identity tag (where it came from) digitally embedded on each video/audio disk, as well as a 'time and date' reference.

Then finally, all the internal data that was downloaded to his department was assigned a location number and then it was retained in a secure area within the basement complex to await final processing.

To do this, it was now up to the individual operators who were trained to deal with this information to look at each and every disk to determine what to do with it before it was put into the retain or destroy category for future assessment, and this assessment depended on whether the conversations and visuals on them had some 'relevance' or was just idle chatter and if this was the case, it was tagged as 'no content' and destined to be destroyed.

These disks were then physically taken to the basement where these disks were then shredded and then melted in a high-temperature oven and the blocks of plastic taken to a disposal facility and shredded into a high-temperature incinerator and destroyed.

Chapter 3

The Real Intent

A long couple of weeks had passed and yet, there was still no sign of what he was hoping to find.

Finally, the weekend was here and it was now pretty late on a Friday.

So far, he had been through and put aside some of the older material from 2000/01 he felt was going to contain something and was about to sign out for a few days off, looking forward to getting home to his family and maybe have some friends over to watch the Packers play the Steelers that night when he looked in the trolley basket and saw that there was only one left.

He picked it up and placed it in his safe as he knew he wouldn't be there for a day or two and the trolley would have to be empty, ready for a whole bunch of new disks from storage for when he got back Wednesday morning.

As he had no time left to start looking at the disk, he put it in his safe and locked it, with the intention of looking at it first thing on his return to the office in a couple of days.

He then picked up his hat and jacket and turned off the lights as he closed the door, and left.

What a great couple of days. The Steelers won, he made a bit of money on the game, and so far, Wednesday looked like a great day, especially as he had an easy run in the traffic to then have it topped off by getting a parking spot right under a tree. So far, so good.

As always, coffee in the canteen then the familiar smell of electronic machinery greeted him on entering his office.

There was the routine of 'booting up' his computer, then setting up the drip coffee machine for a coffee and make a few internal calls to see if all else in his department was as normal too.

He pulled out his bunch of office keys and proceeded to open all the locks in his jurisdiction as well as the safe where he had put the last disk from last week and all the other materials he was to process that day.

But today will not be like the many other of the hundreds of days he had spent here.

As he removed the disk from his drawer, he checked the seal on the disk cover to confirm that it was still intact.

Remembering his reasons for keeping the disk to one side, he broke the seal, slipped it out of its protective envelope and then pushed the disk into the player and waited for it to boot up.

Quickly, he checked all the tags of the disk's encoded reference number and saw that it had not been screened by anyone else as yet.

He let it run.

On his monitor, in the top right-hand corner, the location indicator was flashing on and off. A read-out appeared, showing where it was from.

The Department of Funding and Finance, cam 3/5, 9/11/2001, 8:00 AM – 15:35 PM with the digital clock indicating the date, hour, minute, seconds and meridian at the time of recording.

This particular camera was one of five that were located in various positions both inside and outside this particular room, just like all the others throughout the building, only these were the latest and the smallest cameras installed as part of the building upgrade that had been done to strengthen that side of the building against an external attack, just like the one he was now investigating.

All the cameras in and around all the rooms were all located at exactly the same position in each room.

Camera #1 was at ceiling height, above and opposite the door in the main hall way.

Camera #2 was inside the room, above the door of the entry point to the room and had a 180-degree field of view, which included clear views of the grounds outside the office window.

Cameras #3 and #4, the two most inconspicuous cameras, were high on the internal wall of the office that showed the full panorama view of the desk and part of the area behind the desk where the huge window was, while camera #5 gave a view of much more of the area outside.

This pattern of camera location was standard right throughout the Pentagon.

Bevan could scroll through the vision on the disk with the mouse ball.

This he did to help speed up the tedious process of having to view hours of visuals that at times, had nothing happening or a lot of activity.

It seemed that there was nothing on the disk until at the indicated time of 8:40 AM, when there was a loud noise from the speaker, like a bang in camera 4, the one installed high on an internal wall, there was a rapid flickering of the screen, then it went blank a couple of seconds later.

Curious, Bevan opened the camera 4 screen and began to scroll the visual back to the point where the flickering started, slowly doing frame by frame in reverse, in an effort to get a clear frame that would reveal what had caused the distortion he'd seen.

He went through these frames one by one but nothing was making sense to him at all.

All that he could make out was something moving in the camera's field of view through the window outside, but it was blurred, bright, with little or no discernible form that he could recognise.

Yet, he persisted, as there was something about what appeared through the window view that had a somewhat familiar shape.

The audio was distorted but it sounded like a huge explosive BOOM! that he heard when he saw the screen flicker and go blank.

As he watched the screen, he began to realise that what he was possibly seeing was the initial impact of Flight 77 hiting the Pentagon.

The same aircraft his brother died in on 9/11 before the cameras stopped working.

Bevan, as the head of the security services for communications, was fully briefed about how extensive the system was.

He knew that there was not one square foot of the Pentagon that was not under constant video and audio surveillance as it had been for the last 15 years.

It was obvious to him that somewhere, there was a collection of everything that happened on 9/11 that took place just outside the walls of the Pentagon on that day and he was now more determined than ever to find it, warts and all.

When he realised what he was possibly looking at was the 9/11 attack, he was mortified; he just sat there, moving the frames back and forth in some sort of trance, intently studying each one in fine detail in the hope that maybe, he might catch a glimpse of his brother in one of the windows the moment before he died.

He looked and looked at every frame in that hope, but he could still find no windows, even after he went to the vision from the other cameras.

He didn't see them, even though the images from the door-mounted camera, camera #3, were clearer before it went blank.

He came to the conclusion that there were no windows in any of the hundreds of frames he looked at. Shit!

How come I can't find any windows, he asked himself. Why?

It was then he remembered what he had seen in the 'Loose Change' video, the possibility that it really was a cruise missile, not a 757 that hit the Pentagon after all.

So, he went back to the videos and looked at the footage with a different frame of mind. In doing so, he realised that the shape he had been seeing was really nothing like he thought a large aircraft would look like and was expecting to see. Instead, the bright silver streak he had seen on the security video was small and thin, a similar shape he remembered seeing in the films he'd seen of cruise missiles being launched from B-52s when their tiny thin wings popped out from the side of the missile as it dropped out of the B-52 bomb bay.

Shit, he thought. There has to be more visuals from other cameras of this somewhere in amongst all the other disks in his office, possibly from the rooms where the cameras had been destroyed by the explosion he thought, so he decided to go on a hunt for anything that had the 9/11 date on it, just to make sure if what he'd seen was really what he'd seen.

Even though he was devoted to all that America represents and stands for, Bevan was now starting to have second thoughts about what he had seen in the reported events on TV of 9/11 and what has eventually happened as a consequence since that day.

He knew that whatever he had seen so far, he had to, for the time being, keep it to himself.

As not to alarm any of his staff, he discretely went about securing any and every disk he could find that had the 9/11 in the hope he could make sense of the whole thing that was starting to be revealed to him.

In truth, however, he hoped he was wrong.

In the meantime, as he searched everywhere he could for more information, he went about his job as he always had, attending meetings, briefings, doing training sessions, going to friends for dinner and the occasional party, being the total professional he had always been, cool, amiable, and unflappable.

But day after day, there was always something more he found that had been captured on that fateful day, little snippets that had no direct bearing but enough to start filling in the gaps.

He hoped that eventually, there would be enough of them to help him be able to complete the picture that was emerging.

There were items from all parts of the Pentagon that had some good audio of the impact that seemed to be the same as what he had heard, like a huge explosion that was heard and felt right throughout the complex.

Then there were the reports of the smell of burned cordite (from some Vietnam vets who KNOW what burned cordite smells like), gun smoke from boot camp firing range, a manufactured explosive used in bombs and as the propellant for bullets and artillery shell.

And from all the debriefs of the day, there were no reports of the smell of jet fuel that he knew of.

Even more compelling was the 'in house' visual of people being knocked to the floor of their offices and these reports came from areas that were a long way from the impact zone, indicating the effect of a compression wave from a very large explosion.

It was that particular video that made the biggest impression on him, just as the one from the room he saw first.

The strange thing about the footage of people being knocked over and backwards for quite a considerable distance in the hallways was that it came from a part of the Pentagon complex that was some 200 yards from the point of impact, almost on the opposite side of the building. It made him wonder what it was that had caused that effect.

He remembered when the first "Post-9/11 debrief" at the Pentagon had finished.

He heard snippets of conversations that went on in the officer's dining room and elsewhere, about the strong smell of cordite just like he had smelled.

But many people on the day had said that it was all through the corridors, just minutes after the explosion, and that everyone who was there on that day heard a loud explosion.

But if anything was going to be in the air that day, he reasoned, it would have been the distinctive smell of jet fuel, which is the same smell as kerosene.

However, as much as he could remember, there was no such smell reported by anyone on the day.

Indeed, if, as it was reported, a fully fuelled aircraft supposed to have hit the Pentagon, then the smell of all that burning fuel would have been everywhere!

How come no one smelled it?

Simple logic or common sense would tell you, and it would strongly suggest, that in actual fact, it was rapidly becoming evident that there was no aircraft involved!

Then he came across a security video from the Secretary of Defence Office that proved to be the 'Rosetta Stone' of his search and it terrified him totally.

His monitor showed the usual display of where, when, what time and date it was when recorded.

Sec of Def.-cam 3/5 3/15/98 -8:20AM–4:30PM.

The voices he heard were familiar; he knew them well, not only from the television, but from all the other audio recordings he had already previously classified.

This time, however, he was beginning to hear a different 'tone' , causing him to listen more intently, as it was the first time he had heard these people swearing so profoundly, and their voices were louder and more animated than usual.

So he wondered why.

On his computer monitor were visuals from the Secretary Of Defence office, showing specifically the Secretary of Defence, Dick Chillman with the Deputy Secretary of Defence Saul Alfowitz, both discussing what Bevin now believes were the initial plans for the 9/11 event and this was what happened, in their own words.

Bevan watched and listened.

Just as Paul sat down opposite Dick, he asked, 'Well, what did you think of the proposal"?

Dick said, "Fuck! I always thought you were good, but on this one, I really think that you are out on a limb if this fucks up, because all I can say to you right now is that I appreciate the fact that you and I are members of an exclusive brethren, of men and women who have worked hard and devoted their whole careers in the diplomatic corps, and to make sure that the President is given accurate information at all times, and we have the President's complete trust at all times. But I hope the hell that those you have spoken to in relation to this idea have all given you the undertaking that it must have the consent of the President himself for the final go ahead to have any hope of success, because the agenda to go into Iraq could depend on how others have it presented to them.

Otherwise, we won't be able to get them on our side.

So, other than me, who have you approached and what was their response. ?"

The Deputy SoD, D. Chenly could be seen sitting in a chair on the opposite side of the desk from the Secretary of the DoD, P. Alfowitz, as Alfowitz said, very clearly.

"All of what I have presented here is a result of what the President asked of me in relation to his question when, he asked me point blank.

'What sort of catastrophic event would be needed to effect a regime change in Iraq and get us into the Middle East on a more permanent footing?"

Paul added, "The only people who have any knowledge of it or who I have mentioned it to are you, the Vice President, Andrew Card, the White House Chief of Staff and Secretary of Transportation, David Addington, the White House Chief of Staff and the Department Heads at MASCAL.

You know, the team that conducted two training exercises in January 2000, where a 737 was crashed into this building. I have also spoken to the Air Force chiefs who all said they would be ready to provide the aircraft and tech support we will need.

The Army Chiefs, all of whom are willing to get behind a push for an immediate military response, and anyone who can, I believe, help disguise the fact that we were involved on a first-hand basis.

"And yes, Dick, I am fully aware of what I am saying and doing here, believe me."

Because it is something that has done the rounds here in the Pentagon on a number of occasions over the years but, at those times, they were only exercises.

Paul continued, 'All the Joint Chiefs of Staff and NORAD were conducting all these exercises all over the place.

The last one in '99 was where they used passenger jets as weapons of mass destruction and one more exercise just like it is to happen the day this event is due to happen.

As such, it will be the perfect cover for when it really happens, as all the air cover for this part of the country will be elsewhere on exercise and will be running around like crazy, with everyone wondering if it is yet another exercise or real world.

But the icing on the cake is this.

The Air Force and the Army have put at our disposal, a whole range of facilities we will need when it comes to the relocation of the personnel flying on these aircraft who will need to be 'quarantined' as events unfold, those being all the passengers on the aircraft that are flown under all radar to remote airfields by remote control where these people will be removed and taken to these facilities I was talking about.'

Dick said, "I want to know how far down the road you are with this, because even the pricks down at MASCAL who have been tasked with coming up with all kinds of fucked-up shit dealing with all kinds of scenarios like this would call you a flake, a real loose cannon so to speak, as coming up with a scheme like what you have just put to me now is so out of left field."

"I tell you this."

to even try and imagine that this idea of yours would ever be considered by any sane person or possibly one of the totally flipped out rat bags in MASCAL, is, to me, beyond any rational thought process, as this sort of thinking gets you either shot or put in a room without any windows and rubber walls for the rest of your God dam life!

Know what I mean?

Dick added, ' Paul! Right at this moment, I need some more time to digest this, so, to ask what my response to this will be before I have had time to think about what you have just presented, is premature and unwise.

"So Paul, I need you to get the hell out of my sight, because right now, I want to throw you into the deepest darkest hole I can find."

The recorded images from the pinhole camera number #3 located high in the corner of Dick's office overlooking Dick's desk and office windows then showed Paul leaving the office.

All cameras then showed Dick standing up, walking to his office window that looked towards the capitol building and there, he stood for several minutes, staring out the window, standing still, and it looked like he was taking several deep breaths.

Chapter 4

Understanding

I t was taking shape in Bevan's head now.

What he had been hearing and seeing was the very beginnings of the aerial attacks on 9/11 either being planned or finalized, not by a terrorist group or some backroom cowboys from MASCAL but by our own most senior and trusted government officials, including a future Vice President.

Just like the scenario presented in 'Loose Change' where 'hijacked' aircraft and drones were used to create a situation that would be used to effect a result on the diplomatic front that would secure a more favourable outcome of a dangerous situation developing in Cuba at the time.

As he was sitting at his desk watching all these disks he had put tyo one side for closer scrutiny, he became more convinced about what had been presented in the video, 'Loose Change.' the theory of 911 was being presented as an ' Inside job '

At the time, 911 was being portrayed as a slap in the face of every patriotic American.

He even remembered denouncing the makers of the video as merely attempting to sensationalize and stir up shit.

But now, it seemed to have earned some believability in his eyes.

Now that he had personally seen the internal videos of the day, the internal reports, heard eye witnesses, and saw the injured who came back to work, it was all fitting in neatly with what was put forward in 'Loose Change.'

He was becoming more convinced that what they presented was not that far fetched.

He was also starting to feel that there was something to the 'Loose Change' video that had also made the same suggestion.

But if what they proposed there is actually true, what the hell was it for and did it really mean and maybe, just maybe, these videos are to be the answer to these questions posed right here in the Pentagon?

How ironic that would be, he thought, that the ones who are supposed to be defending us are actually the ones who actually attacked us? JEEZ!

And here he was, looking at the proof it was an 'inside job.'

But what does he do with it and just who does he tell it to to make Americans realise that their government is not what it says it is. ?

Bevan now had to decide what, if anything, he was to do with all the information he had gathered that in his judgement was irrefutable evidence that 9/11 really was an inside job?

He was faced with a monumental dilemma of bringing all this information to the attention of someone he could trust and believe him and the evidence he now has in his possession.

He knew he could suffer enormously and there will be an even larger toll on those who he would have to involve in the scrutiny of this material.

If the original architects of 9/11 ever got wind of what he had in his possession, it would never see the light of day, nor would he.

Because what he has seen and heard on these disks and others was part of the secrecy act and, as a result, he was duty bound to keep it that way.

But deeper inside him was the thought that all the values he had been raised to believe about America, especially her system of government, law and justice, were going to be relegated to the scrap heap if nothing was done.

Right now, even though he didn't know it, he was the only person in America who had the truth in hand and once it was out there, America will have to face the toughest test it has ever faced as a nation.

If it failed to be the holy grail of 9/11, he would become the fall guy, the sacrificial lamb so to speak.

And yet, it was a journey he knew he had to take.

Bevan was entering a state of shock and it made him feel quite ill.

At that moment, he knew that he was also being recorded, too, he knew that if he was to remove any of these disks, it would not be possible to do it here because there was nowhere in his office that was not covered with video surveillance.

It had to be elsewhere. He also knew more than ever that he had to retrieve as many original disks as he could that were proof-dated after the disk he was presently watching and listening.

It's important to isolate as many disks as possible that would expose the activities in the Secretary of Defence's office that he thought would reveal all the dealings on Paul Alfowitz's 9/11.

If he'd succeed, he could find out all the others who were involved, this 'inner circle' of powerful men.

Now that he has seen, heard and stolen this information, he knew he had to develop a plan to get all these disks away from the Pentagon without being caught.

If he was caught, no matter what he said, he would certainly be facing a life term in Leavenworth, branded a traitor.

He had to think hard, especially about what his next step would be and who, if he gets the disks out, could he trust to be shown the content of these DVDs.

He had to find someone who was in a position to do something about it and there was no way in the world he could let this information be swept from history.

If he was caught, every single bit of information that was sitting on the computers at the Pentagon would never see the light of day, as it would all disappear under the most mysterious of circumstances.

He couldn't afford to fail, as the very core of everything about America is recognised and trusted for all over the world must be seen; it had to be held accountable if it is to remain the leader of all that is right and good for all freedom-loving people, or it would never again be in a position of trust.

He must do it now, he thought, just like what PFC Bradley Manning had to do when he saw that someone had, in his opinion, done wrong.

Bevan was sure that the same questions went through

Bradley Manning's mind about who could he trust. Who could he trust to see it through, not only for himself, but for the nation?

Bevan kept asking himself the same question over and over again, and he wondered, 'How can they live with the guilt of what they had done?

Was it just a grab for total control?

Were they just addicted to being in a position of trust and power so badly that they deluded themselves into believing that all their actions, no matter how drastic or destructive, were done in the best interests of the nation, no matter who gets in the way?

Bevan was so deeply moved and offended by their calloused disregard for their fellow Americans' lives, which only galvanized him to make up his mind and finally take action.

However, exactly how he was going to do it was yet to come to mind, but he knew that when it did happen, it will make the world stand still.

But first things first: how does he go about getting these disks out of the Pentagon without getting caught?

He already knew what he would have to face if the people he must trust fail to protect him.

It would be the same fate as PFC Bradley Manning, who sent Wikileaks the video of the massacre of innocent men, women and children by an Apache helicopter crew in Basra.

The driving factor that was to have the greatest influence on his decision was what had happened to Daniel Ellsberg in 1968.

Ellsberg was working for the Rand Corporation where he discovered a series of communication papers from the Pentagon to the White House, addressing the problems the Johnson administration was encountering in South Vietnam and how the war was proving to be 'un-winnable.'

He knew he had to do something so he made some photo copies of them and sent them to the New York Times, which printed them.

The whole thing became known as "The Pentagon Papers," revealing that Lyndon Johnson and his administration were systematically lying to Congress about what was really happening in Vietnam and that it was an un-winnable war.

As a result, the Johnson administration was forced from office, which brought an early end to the war.

Even though Ellsberg was dragged through the courts by the Johnson administration, accusing him of revealing state secrets and being a traitor, common sense and justice were victorious and he wasexonerated.

He was hailed as a hero "for having the guts and fortitude" to bring to the public's notice the wrongs he felt had to be put right.

He proved that even the most powerful men in the land are answerable to the laws of the land and that the Constitution really is worth believing in.

The more he thought about it, the memory of these events gave him heart and hope and the more possible it became in his mind.

Not doing anything would be the worst thing he could do.

Divulging to the public the information he now had was not going to be an easy task in any way, shape, or form.

But mostly, he was concerned about how he would do it, because it really was the right thingto do.

Should Wikileaks get it?

Or the people who made 'Loose Change'?

Or maybe hack the system himself and "leak" it all to the press?

But doing it like that, how would he cover his tracks?

After all, as he was the head of data security, and he was the only one who would know where this information came from.

Worse, his head would roll further than anyone else's as he is also the one who built the firewall to protect everything here and he is the only one who could get past it and the only one who had access to these disks.

Deep in his heart, though, he knew he had to "blow the whistle."

To keep his thinking on track, he kept reminding himself 'The Oath of Allegiance' and what it meant to him, especially now.

How he recited it every day at school and college and, in particular, the oath he took when he joined the Air Force, "To keep all he heard and saw, secret."

But right now, he felt an anger in his chest like he had never felt before.

Angry that saying nothing would be breaking a thousand laws, but saying nothing would also mean that he was no longer a patriot and would, by his in-action, be complicit in the most heinous of crimes ever perpetrated against America and all Americans and, in particular, the way of life

Americans have enjoyed and taken for granted since the very foundation of the United States of

America as a nation in 1776.

What Bevan had done was pinpoint all the activities of Dick Chillman and who he contacted after he heard the plan he was presented with.

Now that he has accessed all the records from the Secretary of the Department of Defence without setting off any alarms, it was now imperative that it be made public as soon as he could.

Bevan believed he was now obligated to do so.

He was constantly haunted by the images of the moment he saw on TV, the aircraft smashing into the WTC.

And yet, in a strange way, it all seemed to get clearer in his mind, what he knew he had to do.

He was pretty sure that he could do it, just how and when was the problem, but he said to himself, 'There has to be a beginning, so, let's roll!'

America has never been the same since 9/11 and America would never be the same again.

But once the American public becomes aware of the facts about how 9/11 really happened and how it was all perpetrated by these men, she will regain her trusted position in the free world once again, hopefully stronger, for showing that she had some weaknesses and that she rectified it, as painful as it may be.

Once again, all Americans will share in the joy of knowing that the Constitution is still worth putting all their trust and faith in again because it has true meaning.

'Here, what's this pretty chest, then? ' asked the new king, and what's inside it, fool?'

'Oh, sire' said the tiny gnome, 'this box belongs to a friend of mine and her name is Pandora, and sire, she has told me that if anyone should open it in her absence, a spell that has been locked inside for the last hundred years will escape, and a calamity like the Earth has never seen before will be released and will destroy everyone and everything in it! '

"Baah, humbug! I don't believe in spells and the like said the new king. 'Just open it!' 'But sire!"

Chapter 5

A Little Bit of History

Just prior to the 9/11 attacks, America was in crisis.

Bevan, with his head in his hands, was more aware of the dire situation than most.

Every hour of every day, the extent of discontent that raged around the globe was growing.

The list of potential threats seemed to get longer every day, with more and more information being fed into the system from agents and embassies all over the world on a continual basis.

But now, all the things out there that posed a threat to the United States of America should be of no concern to any one at the moment as it was becoming clearer to him that all the "discontent" was being manufactured and used by the government spin doctors as a tool to shift blame and gain social control.

Russia was a good old reliable source of keeping us scared, 24/7, to deliberately disguise the real events and especially to justify on a daily basis America's ongoing presence and war in Iraq and in Afghanistan, too. But according to Donald Dumsfeld and his network of friends, it's all because of the events that took place on 9/11, serving as justification for America to be at war in the Middle East.

Commerce was fully aware, too, that on the world stage and, more directly, on the domestic front, the United States of America was in bad shape.

It has had its embassies become targets for bombings by radical Muslims.

There was OPEC and its pricing of oil beyond what was once reasonable.

North Korea was flexing its atomic muscles, and now this: how would America and her people handle this revelation now that there was a new President, a man who wanted truth in government?

Well, let's see how he deals with this lot, Bevan thought, as the hard yards were about to start. He found it difficult at first to take into consideration the fact that Dick had spent his whole life as a public servant and that the release of this material will mean that Dick Chillman's life and all those who were involved, especially the Bush family, would be destroyed.

But all those concerns disappeared from his mind the more he heard and saw what was on the disks.

But how in God's name did they think that something like this could be held a secret?

And where and who were all the innocents that got caught up in something they had no control over?

That was the sad part—all the dead!

As stated in "Loose Change," the story of "Operation Northwood" was the last time a suggestion like this was made to a President, but it got the man fired, never to be part of the career path he'd chosen ever again, being put in a metaphorical desert…for life.

That person being Admiral Lembitzer in 1963, and Dick was part of the White House staff back then.

As he was preparing to take his plans to the President, little did he know at the time that President George W Bush Jr had already been briefed about the planned 9/11 attack and was already in it up to his armpits, as well as the rest of the Bush family!

It seemed that every intelligence agency in the free world was humming with activity on all levels, in the hope that any new threat or planned terrorist act could be intercepted and acted on before the terrorist organizations could act, but Dick made the call to Paul, anyway, to ask him to report to his office as soon as possible.

The FBI, CIA, and the Department of Defence analysts are always working overtime, working at finding and, if need be, preventing from ever happening again anything like what had happened in Africa or the bombing of the World Trade Centre basement in 1993.

America and the free world and those who call themselves allies of the US were all led to believe that the greatest threat that had ever been presented before was in the Middle East and all the intelligence gathered so far indicated that the greatest "perceived" threat came from those who controlled the oil output, production, and pricing.

As of 2011, all the world media outlets were told by the American government spin machine that, according to all these intelligence gathering agencies, America's security at home and abroad was constantly under threat.

These threats seemed to be coming from these current hot spots, which were Afghanistan and Iran and, to a greater degree, North Korea.

Pre-9/11, Americans were starting to hear stories about the most savage man in the world, Saddam Hussein.

Intense focus of the American intelligence gathering agencies was on Saddam Hussein, the ruthless and utterly corrupt dictator of Iraq who had sent his army into Kuwait to capture the country's oil processing and shipping facilities.

Unfortunately for Saddam, his army was roundly defeated by America because the world was told by the Bush spin doctors that the Iraqi army was killing babies in the kuwait Hospital by throwing them out of their humidicribs and leaving them on the floor to doe, as they were taking these humidicribs back to Iraq.

All these stories turned out to be total bullshit that was used by Bush as leverage to get America a base in the Middle East.

In one of the videos that astounded many was the, daughter of the Kuwait's ambassador's to America, telling the US Congress how Iraqi soldiers were seen throwing babies on the floor of the hospital in their quest to take the "incubators" back to Iraq.

Something GHW Bush put to the American public as God's truth and presented in such a way as a case for why America must see Saddam Hussein removed from power.

All lies.

All with crocodile tears, all to pull at the heart strings of Mr and Mrs America—and it worked, as the young girl was coached by some American publishing enterprise on how to deliver her story.

With the Bush senior administration securing the bases in 1991 in the Middle East it always wanted, declaring war on Iraq, all based on this young girl's false claims.

So, these lies were being believed by the world (because America said so), America was increasingly putting herself in the position of starting and establishing a military presence in the Middle East, the likes of which had never been possible before but had always wanted, and now, they have got it!

Meanwhile, in Afghanistan, Osama Bin-Laden, the billionaire heir to the construction company owned by his family from Oman, was becoming the financier and the spiritual figurehead of a terrorist group with training camps in both Afghanistan and Pakistan, calling itself Al-Qaeda.

According to the information given to President GHW Bush by his department heads and diplomats, Bin-Laden was preparing his group to become the "mother of all terrorist groups" until he was eliminated by Obama's hit men.

Pre-9/11, with these two becoming the focus of this attention, thoughts turned to creating a regime change in Iraq and somehow overthrow its dictator.

This line of thinking made Bin-Laden the prime target of the US administration as he was supposedly linked to the bombings of the American embassies on the African continent.

He was indeed someone they could "blame and go after."

That was in the 1980s and George Bush Sr was president.

He was the first to take action against Osama Bin-Laden for those attacks on American embassies. However, Bush failed to get him with a number of cruise missile strikes on what he'd been told were the training camps that Bin-Laden had established, high in the mountains of Afghanistan.

To all the people who knew the Bush family, that was a really strange thing to do, as the Bin-Laden family were personal friends of the Bushes.

Somehow, the American agencies were informed in a French intelligence report that was also given to the online publication of The Guardian Unlimited by Anthony Sampson on 1 November 2001, stating that Osama Bin-Laden had received medical treatment in an American hospital in Dubai on 4/7/2001, for 10 days after flying in from Quetta in Pakistan with his own personal doctor, nurses and four bodyguards.

He was apparently treated in the urology department, where several members of his immediate family also visited him and he was also visited by the local chief of the CIA, even though he was on America's wanted list since 1998.

French intelligence was keen to disclose the ambiguous role of the CIA and used all its persuasion to restrain Washington from extending the war into Iraq and elsewhere.

Unfortunately, America, the land of the free and the home of the brave, was rapidly gaining a tarnished reputation, being branded as a den of liars and neoconservatives with an agenda to have it's presence and influence in the name of peace and democracy felt in all parts of the world, no matter what the cost.

Mostly by using its military might to achieve these aims and with statements like 'New World Order' ringing in people's ears, there was more and more direct resistance to these attempts to "democratize" the world.

This was most especially apparent in the Middle East, where America had to become more vigilant in its efforts to protect its interests there as well as in other locations around the world, and it's now a continual pattern of 'history repeating itself.'

Since the predicted peak of oil production in the early 1970s and the impending oil shortage that spawned a whole new way of transporting the world in smaller and more economical cars, America's manufacturing base had taken a decided downturn.

Consequently, America started looking at what measures she would have to implement that would safeguard its future energy needs and supplies.

As 90% of all her energy requirements at that time came from the Middle East, the radical changes that had started taking place there over the last 10 years was of a major concern to the power brokers and all who were in the business of trading all these commodities on Wall Street, legally and illegally.

The Bush administration was especially wary when it came to the noticeable increase of the Muslim influence that was starting to make a big impact on the policies being developed by these Middle Eastern leaders, Saddam Hussein in particular.

Saddam Hussein, even though he was best mates with Donald Dumsfeld, was making a name for himself as far back as the early 1980s with his ruthless and deadly way of continually being at war with Iran for five years with the loss of hundreds of thousands of his troops, then his deadly suppression of the dissenting Shia Arabs of northern Iraq, with poison gas.

World opinion really started to turn against him when he gassed a whole town of Kurds in the north, killing thousands of men, women, and children.

There was also the brutal and deadly way he put down the uprising in the south after the invasion of Kuwait—the invasion that was stopped by American liberating forces that pushed the invading Iraqi army back over the border.

Yeah, God bless America.

Chapter 6

The Kitchen

The American government spin doctors were starting to have an impact on world opinion with stories about weapons of mass destruction.

On everyone's mind, due to the concerted efforts of the media and newspapers reporting of the invasion of Kuwait, these stories were now being believed.

Especially when the likes of the former Army General, Colin Howell, and Paul Alfowitz stood before the General Assembly of the United Nations and said, along with glossy eight-by-ten-inch photos from their spy satellites, that it was fact.

World leaders then started putting their support behind America's idea that change had to take place in Iraq and quickly, as the whole world was to suffer if nothing was done to rid the world of this mad man and his weapons of mass destruction (WMDs).

Little did the world know that right from the first shot fired in the 'Liberation of Kuwait', there were men plotting the invasion, battle plans, logistics and everything else America will need when the total invasion of Iraq happens.

But how do they get the mandate they need from the American public to invade another country when there had really been no provocation from the one they wanted to invade?

Simple: just tell lies, more lies and more damned lies.

And how would they convince the world that it is the right thing to do?

It would have to be, as one general said.'a second Pearl Harbour'.

It would have to be done with an almighty bang.

But how and when it would be done was the biggest problem on Dick's mind.

The radical suggestion by Paul was as crazy as it gets.

But if they could get the American public's support and sympathy, they would then be in a position to break out of Kuwait and invade Iraq.

Bevan was now in possession of more and more recordings that took place in not only the Secretary of Defence's office, but it was becoming obvious that many others were involved, not directly but, in the roundabout way that Dick liked to conduct business with his staff, be they civilian or military personnel, and the details on those disks were shocking, in the cold-blooded way they planned and discussed the impending deaths of innocent people with complete disdain.

Dick had Paul come back and repeat, in the finest detail, all of what he had said earlier that morning.

Dick made the call and within 15 minutes, Paul was back in Dick's office and outlined everything to Dick in fine detail.

'OK, Paul, what I have decided to do is talk to some people I believe will be willing to look at your proposal. What you will have to realise, Paul, is that this is so similar to 'Operation Northwood, uncanny."

'Dick, I have read all there is to know on Northwood and all the scenarios dealing with 'aircraft as missiles' that I could find. I am well prepared for what is about to happen here, as I have been working on this plan since the truck bomb was detonated in the basement of the World Trade Centre in '93 and the liberation of Kuwait.

"You know better than most, Dick, that the Pentagon is more than capable of creating a secret and bloody war of terror, be it against their own country in order to trick the American public into supporting a war on terrorism in Iraq or Afghanistan, or even the invasion of Cuba, if need be."

If this can be done, then the invasion of Iraq will be the direct response to these attacks, as part of the agenda to assert the US presence there so that the US can put in place the agenda that was first derived by the first Bush administration and is wanted by the current President more than ever before' , 'at all costs' as he put it.

Paul then said, 'It was after the truck bomb of 1993 when I was asked to attend a luncheon with

Larry Gullverstein and the New York Port Authority bosses to discuss what security measures were to be taken to ensure that any future threat to the complex would be detected before anything could ever happen again.

In the address to the Port Authority and guests, Jerry went to some length in his address saying that the buildings were fast approaching their 'use-by date.' Mr. Gullverstein also outlined what the next phase of development would be that was scheduled for the WTC complex and that it was not that many years off.

He discussed how he would have to seriously consider removing the two buildings that are the tallest in the world with explosives, to make way for new ones."

Paul then went on to explain what he suggested. "It was at this moment that I saw the opportunity to create the second 'Pearl Harbour.'

The incident I was looking for that would help sway American opinion to have a reason to invade Iraq and it was after the luncheon with these thoughts in mind that I made an indirect comment to Larry to the effect that, 'What would happen if a wayward airplane lost in the fog hits one of them?

Or if a suicide attack in a hijacked plane was to happen, we could blame it on terrorists.

Would your insurance provider cover you against that sort of thing?'

Because I am sure that would certainly solve your problem of how to get them down and you might even make enough money from it, to build a new complex.

'Even though I was deadly serious, I said it in such a way that it sounded like a smart-assed joke, and I laughed' said Paul. "Mr Gullverstein just stood there with a very concerned look on his face, and said, 'Are you fucking serious?'

And all I could do was shrug my shoulders and give him a wink.

'This was when I started to fine tune my plans that would effectively start the unstoppable momentum for the regime change he felt was necessary in Iraq'.

"Over the next couple of months, I had quite a few meetings with Mr Gullverstein, under the pretext of new infrastructure subsidies loans that we could make available for any new projects planned for the WTC, such as for replacement of all the fire-proofing asbestos on all the steel frames under the floor of every level, something Larry was not willing to undertake due to the cost of removing the old covering before the new material was installed, so demolition was the only option.'

'I was feeling very confident that my ideas of what I had in mind was something that was going to succeed and it was really starting to take shape but what I didn't know at the time was that the Federal Government had many of its departments located in building 7 of the WTC, some of those being the CIA, the Secret Service, and Mayor Giuliani's emergency bunker.

It's also where the SEC stores three to four thousand files related to numerous Wall Street investigations about irregularities in the trading practices of some trading houses.

"Mr Larry Gullverstein, the then-owner of the whole WTC complex, would eventually take out a 99- year lease worth 3.2 billion dollars on the WTC just six weeks before 9/11 but on July 24 th , 2001 he also took out an insurance policy that included clauses related to 'terrorist attacks' on the whole complex on which he stood to collect 3.5 billion dollars if the complex suffered an attack by 'terrorists', and this was, I believe, was the result of the conversation we had just before I came back to Washington after the luncheon in New York."

Paul continued explaining to Dick, saying, 'It was after the Supreme Court challenge to the vote counting system in Florida that found in favour of Mr George Bush Jr over Gore, giving him the Presidency, that I thought my idea may have a sympathetic ear, so to speak, because it was then that the newly elected President Bush Jr asked me what sort of catastrophic event would be needed to effect a regime change in Iraq.

As his dad had been held back by Congress due to the fact there was no mandate to continue on after Kuwait when he had the chance, but didn't have the ok from Congress until the UN was informed of what the US knew about them to go after him at all.

Even with babies being removed from their stolen humidicribs by Iraqi soldiers who reportedly threw these babies on the hospital floor to die, it still was not enough probable cause.

So then, WMDs were the spin we were fed.

'I am sure you remember the open letter that was sent to President Ninton by the members of 'The New American Century,' challenging him to act forcefully and militarily to remove Saddam Hussein from power and how nothing was done except that he sent you there to try and effect a halt in his aggression against Iran.

'Well, after that, I started to investigate who was sympathetic in their thinking in having Saddam removed from power and how they would go about it.

Unsurprisingly, I came across many people in the present and past administrations who are willing to go along with a stronger American presence in the Middle East, even 'at the end of a gun'.

I was told by all of them that he must be confronted directly, but it would take a very persuasive president with a wealth of irrefutable information.

The results of a poll taken after Kuwait's liberation indicated that Americans had had enough of our troops being on foreign soil and it was too soon after Grenada, Haiti, Bosnia, and some even said Vietnam, to be involved in a war where we were the sole participants.

Besides, we don't want a repeat of the 1970s when anti-war protesters and dissidents ruled the day.

"So for America to be engaged in a protracted military action in Iraq, it would have to be a most significant event that would trigger the sort of reaction that would have Americans screaming for blood.

But what would be needed is 'a second Pearl Harbour,' an event so horrific that it would give the Bush administration the mandate to go to war.

'Once it was proved that all the intelligence gathered pointed directly at what we want the world to look at, the rest of the world would beat a path to our door, offering assistance in bringing down this tyrant Hussein and the terrorist organization he supports.

Leaders of democratic countries that were sympathetic to America's plight would be more inclined to 'form a coalition of force' rather than see this tyrant perpetuate more fear than he was already party to.

'This could only be done, with the support of the UN. I am sure that you have read through the early files of the Kennedy Administration, as you were a member of the White House staff in those days'.

You would have had to come across 'Operation Northwood' where Admiral Liman Dimnitzer, the then-chairman of the Joint Chiefs of Staff, came up with a plan that was presented to Robert MacNamara, the then-Secretary of Defence, on March 13, 1962?'

'Yeah, I remember when Macartney presented it to President Kennedy who rejected it and then personally fired the Admiral, but the proposed plan in itself was a good one.

And if my memory is good, we were to stage terrorist attacks in and around Guantanamo Bay (American soil) and to use two aircraft that were painted to look like commercial jets, I think, one of which would be full of CIA agents but made to look like they were all college students on their way to Jamaica for their summer break or something like that'. 'But in reality, one of these aircrafts was an unmanned drone'.

The drone and the one with real people on it would have dual registration, and they would exchange mid-flight with the drone that flies on over Cuban waters where it sends a 'Mayday' as it was being attacked by a Cuban Air Force jet, right?

But is to be actually destroyed with explosives via a radio signal or something like that, I think, and all done to provide a pretext for military intervention in Cuba. Yeah, fucki'n brilliant.'

Paul said,"So, for the US to have a permanent presence in the Middle East, what I have in mind issomething similar ".

"It would have to be a catastrophic event that would happen right here in America, an event that would be automatically made to look like a terrorist attack, where we will be capable of providing proof of them entering the country and being in the country months before it happened, with visuals of them at various airports preparing to do it, backed up by the media who will say and do everything we want them to do, as saying or doing anything else would be 'un-patriotic'".

"The intention is to make it look like a group of about seven to ten men of Middle Eastern appearance arrive in America over a short period of time, creating for them a timeline of activities that will include getting some experience in various light aircraft as well as a flight simulator for passenger type aircraft, something they will prove somewhat 'clumsy' and somewhat nervous at, according to the pilots that 'trained' them while they were here."

"There will be a paper trail of them being here, too, such as letters from their 'handlers' in the Middle East, instructions for the day with dates, time, and places it is all to happen at and what airports will be involved, etc."

"Two aircraft would be flown into the World Trade Centre early in the morning, followed by one flying into the Pentagon within the following hour, with a fourth being flown towards the Capitol that would be shot down but be made to look like the passengers tried to stop the hijackers by deliberately crashing the jet through a violent fight with the 'terrorists' in the cockpit."

"It's common knowledge that commercial aircraft can be flown as radio controlled drones via a secure radio link.

This was developed by Raytheon after there were quite a few hijackings of aircraft in the 1970's, so that the control of these aircraft could be taken out of the hands of the pilots on board, to prevent the airplane from crashing and to be able to land the aircraft where we wanted it to land and deal with the hijackers."

"A drone aircraft was flown with great success on 1/12/1984 when there was a remote-controlled

Boeing 707 that took off from the Edwards Air Force base and was crash landed by NASA for raw fuel combustion research."

But before it was destroyed, they had flown it a total of sixteen hours and twenty-two minutes, which included, ten take offs, sixty-nine approaches, and thirteen landings."

The drone aircraft to be used for the attack on the WTC will be 757's, all painted to look like commercial passenger aircraft, and will be fitted with tube-launched missiles that are in conformal pods that lay flush with the fuselage, barely noticeable to the untrained eye."

These missiles will be fired milliseconds before the aircraft hits the target and will start the jet fuel burning immediately to create a huge fireball explosion on impact."

"When it comes to providing fighters to shoot down these 'hijacked aircraft,' there simply won't be any around on that day because the air force (NORAD) will be on an exercise at the other end of the country, like Texas or Alaska, where the hijacked aircraft were to be flown into government controlled installations."

"To ensure that the 'attacks' will succeed, the other elements of the Air Force base close to Washington would be sent to Alaska for an exercise there."

"In August 1999, we were to conduct an exercise where airliners were flown into the WTC, but was knocked on the head because defence officials said that it was 'unrealistic' to do so."

"Do you remember being part of the two exercises in October 2000 called 'Nascow' when a scenario was run that had a 737 fly into the Pentagon using a huge architectural model where it had a broken model of a 737 sitting on the ground in the 'inner ring." ?

"When I attended the luncheon in New York about the redevelopment of the WTC, Larry Gullverstein also gave me the contact details of a specialist demolitions company who 'asks no questions,' who will be able to give us more precise information on how the buildings would be set up for demolition, as he had hired them before to remove some other building complexes ready for new ones."

"They are 'Controlled Demolitions', Inc. and it's run by a Mr Mark Bizeaux."

As I just said, he has done some work for Larry when he was involved in some redevelopment projects.

Larry said he could be trusted to make all the arrangements, and if need be, explain exactly what will happen to make the building collapse straight down, in a pancake fashion, that would minimises the damage to the buildings nearby.

"When it comes to gaining access to the WTC complex, all the security systems at the World Trade Centre are controlled by President Bush's brother Jeb's company, as he is head of security for the whole complex and he also is in control of all the security nationwide, at American Airlines, so getting the technicians into the WTC complex to set the charges won't be a problem ".

"As for access to airport facilities, it would be the same arrangements there, too."

"Do you have a particular time of day for this to happen?"

"What are the expected casualties, if any, will there be?"

"There will be some people still in the towers trapped by the damage cause, but after the first aircraft goes in, it only stands to reason that everyone who is in them will instinctively want to get out of the buildings."

"I can't be totally sure of how many people will die in the initial attacks, as it will take some time before the buildings are bought down and in that time, all the WTC complex hopefully will have been completely evacuated by the various response teams, such as the fire fighters, police and the Port Authority Security police."

"'Obviously, there will be some deaths due to the 'attack', and that will be unfortunate but we must think of what America stands to gain."

"So, I believe, that with the right spin, the death toll will fade into insignificance and people will grieve but will feel vindicated when we 'get the bastards who did this'."

"By then, we will have given the world all the reasons to join us after they are shown the 'evidence' that Saddam Hussein supported the terrorist's in their attack on America and that he poses a real threat to the world."

'What about the Pentagon?'

"Well, all the information I can gather without raising any red flags tells me that the accuracy in flying radio-guided drones is not an exact science, so there will have to be other arrangements made that will increase the impact effect, which will give the impression of a huge and destructive impact on the side of the building I believe should be targeted, but as for casualties in the Pentagon won't be as severe as the WTC casualty numbers, but there will be some deats and injuries for sure and that is unfortunate."

"I am looking at actually using a cruise missile here, and a large amount of C4 that was installed in the area of impact will go off the second the missile hits."

"This is because, getting a commercial-size aircraft that low and have a remote guidance pilot put it exactly in the side of the Pentagon could fail in the sense that there could be some very important and vital personnel killed if it missed the targeted part of the building."

"Also, I want the impact point to be where it was recently upgraded to withstand exactly this sort of incident ".

"On the day, I will have it arranged so that all the offices there will have very few or no people, as at the moment it's mostly domestic services in that area."

"Any video cameras that face that side of the building will be out of order on the day and for those on private property near the Pentagon, they will have members of the FBI turn up and remove the tape, along with the standard warnings about national security and such."

"OK, will the hits on the WTC be more precise? '

"How will it be done and could these aircraft actually bring down the building? '

"Yes to both questions, and from my communications with Mr Gullverstein, he has assured me that he is currently making all the necessary arrangements with the demolition engineers and has already approached the New York mayor's office indicating that he will be seeking permission from them at a later date for a go-ahead with the planned controlled demolition of the WTC at some time in the not-too-distant future to make way for the new structures."

"From what Mr Gullverstein says, this information was released deliberately so that they would be able to effectively set in place the material and manpower who will be doing the preparation that will affect the total collapse of the WTC without raising any concerns from its occupants and tenants."

"And with Jeb Bush, the President's brother being the head of security for the WTC, there is an assurance there that Silverstein will be able to have all the security systems shut down at the times the demolition technicians are actually working in these buildings setting the charges so that there will be no interruptions or unwanted questions being asked by people who may see these men working in the buildings ".

"Seeing strangers walking through the building at all hours of the day may raise some alarm, but the alibi would be an 'ongoing computer cabling upgrade' to increase internet speed."

"Needless to say, these men will have unhindered access to all areas at all hours of the day."

"Jeb also told Gullverstein that he has personally made arrangements for the explosives-sniffing dogs that usually accompany the security staff on their rounds to be removed from service."

"These drone aircraft will have the transponder shut down not long after take-off and will be fitted with a laser guidance system, similar to the cruise missile guidance system linked to the flight control fly by wire system."

"The laser designators will be located on the roofs of some derelict buildings on the Lower East Side, and one will be set up on the West Side to guide the first aircraft in."

"All of them are a good distance from the towers and will have a clear line of sight to put a beam on the building, enabling the receiver on the aircraft to lock onto it a long way out and will fly straight and steady and impact exactly on the mark the designator is aimed at—almost surgical, you might say."

"This means that we can then order all airborne aircraft to land immediately and have the duplicate aircraft with the passengers that the drones are replacing be flown below any radar coverage to a pre-determined secure location where, after landing, they will be immediately parked in hangars where they can't be seen from the air."

"After the aircraft have been parked in a secure area, the passengers, after being told of the events that have just happened in New York are to be taken and placed in a facility while security checks are done on the aircraft they were on before they will be allowed to continue their journey ".

"These passengers will then be removed and taken by vehicles disguised as army trucks with Spanish insignia on them to a secure facility, where they will be processed like they have been landed in what will look like to them, a foreign country, such as Cuba."

"In reality, these are the new facilities built by Homeland Security to house any future dissidents or foreign combatants, 'for processing', but in the meantime, we will be using them to house the passengers so that we can keep a lid on what has really happened."

"The 'staff' in these facilities will give the passengers the impression that they are local military personnel that can't speak English and will not communicate with the people who have just arrived but will only indicate where the soldiers want the passengers to go with gestures."

"These members of ' staff' will have been trained to behave like foreign soldiers in a way it won't look suspicious, because in reality, they are involved in the training of US military personnel for being on foreign soil.

"I don't know if you are aware of it, but it is now possible to block any mobile phone and internet access on board these aircraft and it will make sure that there will be no information in or out."

"These passengers will be told that there are no mobile phone or internet facilities in this country yet, and all the windows on these particular aircraft will have been especially modified, where the windows can be 'fogged' so that the passengers can't see or possibly recognize any landmarks or anything that may give them any idea of where they really are."

"There is also technology available where we can create in the families' minds the impression that they have received a phone call from their son or daughter or wife or husband on any one of these aircraft by cross-referencing the names on the passenger list with the personal information they have all previously provided that is currently held on a database in Washington."

"All the passengers from these aircraft will have the same experience once they have landed and been removed from the aircraft, being placed on vehicles and removed from these 'airports' under the pretext that the aircraft were hijacked."

"They will be led to think they are now on foreign soil and will be taken to a holding facility, where they will be safe and secure and eventually will be repatriated back to the US once a time and place can be arranged for their release."

"Once these people are secure and incommunicado in these facilities, they will be told of the attacks in the US and that there will be a longer-than-expected delay due to the emergency and as a result of that, they will then be taken to a processing centre then a hospital for a quick medical assessment before their flight back to the USA."

"This processing centre is where they will be interviewed by 'Embassy officials,' then medically examined at the hospital and all will be given some medication (to help them sleep that night). In reality, the drug administered to them will put them in an altered state of mind so that they will be totally controlled and then, where and when, will be permanently isolated, one by one, to prevent any 'break' in the chain, so to speak."

"Because, if one of them gets to contact the outside world, the whole thing could be blown wide open and besides, they were literally dead from the first second this plan goes into action any way."

"At these airbases, these passengers will be 'processed' and, to further reinforce in their minds that they really are on foreign soil, unknown to them, their real identity documents will be replaced with pre-fabricated identities."

"From there, they will be selectively distributed to the facilities the government have been building as part of the new prison update programme where they will remain for the rest of their lives.

"The administration staff who will be running these facilities will have, on their computer systems, false intelligence on each one of these persons, misleading these staff members to believe that these new inmates have arrived there as part of the health department's new strategy to house mentally ill patients in more efficient and wholesome surroundings."

"And as patients transferred from other various mental institutions, it will be more readily believed that their behaviour will be seen as a group of patients that are on the new programme."

"Paul, how do you propose to avoid any investigation that could implicate us, or a finding that we were responsible for what you are advocating here, provided it should actually get the support you envisage, and why. ?"

"Well, when it comes to the work done in preparation for the WTC for demolition, the staff who set these charges will be told that it was nothing to do with them as the terrorist attack was a surprise and the fact that there were explosives in the buildings was purely coincidental."

"Regardless of the presence of the explosives, if anyone says that they heard explosions or saw explosions going off after the aircraft hit, it was the impact of the jets that actually started the explosion process happening."

"No matter what is seen or heard, it can all be explained away by saying that the impact set off some explosive charges that had been placed ready for the demolition months before and the fire got so hot that it caused parts of the steel to melt and as a result of the explosives and the fire, it caused the buildings to fall."

"If the press decide that they will go after Gullverstein, they will find all of his bases covered due to the application to council that was made and approved some 12 months before."

"We will use some old security video from the airports these 'terrorists' will fly out of before they hijack the planes so that the world will also get to see the 'terrorists' getting on the aircraft at the airports and hear 'phone calls' from passengers on these flights that will give everybody the impression that it really was a terrorist attack on America."

"You just have to take a walk down memory lane and see the history pages of all the 'activities' that we have been involved in since the days of the Nazis and the Bush family, the attempt to take out Gadhafi in 1980 in the Mediterranean, and especially, the "Warren Report" and the Kennedy assassination as well as all the 'false flag' shit we did."

"It was all the turmoil and confusion that surrounded those events that says it all, as it clearly outlines what I have believed for years now."

"The government's spin on what happened on those occasions was so convincing that it created total confusion on everyone's minds, that even the truth got in the way to the point that no one believed any of it."

"Any witnesses that had anything to offer and looked credible never got to say anything because they met with an 'accident' or died of some mysterious physical ailment before they could appear before any inquiry."

"Anyone who did have something to say or an opinion to offer were totally discredited by their peers and howled down by public opinion and the press, because they were so engrossed in making their careers pay off that they avoided everything that would have had an adverse effect on their careers, their family's safety, and their lives."

Chapter 7

The Exit

Bevan was now due for discharge from the Air Force in less than a year and was constantly being asked by senior officers to consider signing on for six more years, as he had proved to all who knew him that he was an exemplary officer, held in high regard by his peers.

If he chose to stay, he would be part of the planning of strategies, plus a promotion to general.

But in his usual way, he was extremely diplomatic in his responses to his peers' approaches and encouragement to stay, but politely maintained the fact that he would be on a salary with Honeywell that would offer him the lifestyle he had always promised his family once he was in civvy street.

Indeed, he had made up his mind to move on.

One thing in his favour was that since he had been the head of data security at the Pentagon, there had never been any concerns raised about him or his staff, or the way all the data had been handled or processed since he developed the "firewall" he implemented some three years ago.

There were one or two occasions when he had some blank DVDs in his briefcase that he deliberately took home, as a test of the metal detection devices that were at all entrances into and out of the Pentagon.

They were supposed to detect the smallest amounts of anything that contained metal and trigger an alarm, but thankfully, there was a lot of "brass" that went through these portals on an almost continual basis, 24 / 7 and because of that and the fact that everyone there were nearly all on a 'first name basis' of recognition by the personnel who operated these devices, making the number of 'checks' conducted was minimal and the detectors were not at all sensitive to the new 'silver dollar disks' as they became known to the staff.

More of them were taken home as part of the "pen in the pocket" losses than sheets of paper, because the disks were so good and could store all the music anybody could wish for on one disk.

Getting the information out he was gathering may not be a difficult thing, but being stopped was a risk and it still terrified him, as the results would be deadly, literally.

His biggest concern since he decided on the future direction he was on, was to be and to remain 'invisible' if he was to secure the information that would bring these men to justice.

Always in the back of his mind was the fact that due to the nature of what he does on a daily basis, it was important to his employer, the US government, that all security personnel be audited from time to time, such as those concerning their movements, their phone calls, internet logs, and travel and social activities, all with the aim of maintaining the level of secrecy needed by the most paranoid government in the world, a government that had a lot to keep under the carpet.

These audits he found out were conducted by both the FBI and the CIA.

Thankfully, for Bevan, it was not seen as unusual for him to be ordering so many blank DVDs on his request forms to stores each month, as he was constantly making duplicates of the DVDs he'd been classifying that were then sent to the USCDL after the final OK by Dick Cheney himself, all on a daily basis.

So his duplication of the 9/11 disks was so far not raising any questions. Everything was on track and actually ahead of schedule.

The only one he was answerable to was his immediate boss, Donald Ruskin, the Secretary of Defence.

Mr Ruskin was the only one who gives the go ahead to the transfer of the data after classification each day before it is sent to the US Congressional Digital Library, and there lay the biggest obstacle in his intentions to make the information public.

Knowing that, Bevan made sure that the DVDs of what happened in the Secretary of Defence office over that period of time would eventually be put before Mr Ruskin for his OK to have it transferred to the library, and Bevan was also sure that Donald Ruskin would be fully aware of the fact that all that happened in his office would eventually be read by somebody somewhere down the road.

Bevan deliberately delayed passing the DVDs to the secretary by having them earmarked for release at a much later date, well after his discharge was effected.

Keeping up the appearance of a man in control for all around him all came to an end on the 15th of March 2010, but it became the day that he had to start the inevitable journey he embarked on when he discovered, quite by a twist of fate, what really happened, on 9/11/01 and, how it was done.

Chapter 8

The Quiet

Paranoia is not in Bevan's vocabulary, but as cautious as he had been about who to trust, he had finally made the decision of what he would have to do and who to contact to effect his promise to America, his brother and especially, his own family.

On the day he first discovered the conspiracy, he made a promise to himself that he would not involve them in any way whatsoever and, even if he wanted to tell anyone, let alone a member of his family, he couldn't, as he was bound by the secrecy act and the oath he took.

But that may all change as a greater sense of reassurance he is doing the right thing will come into play.

He had resolved that they would all remain innocent and blameless and, if his future actions failed to get a response from the people he was going to have to trust to tell his story, any investigations into his actions would reveal that they were all completely unaware of his discovery.

Besides, he never even spoke to any of his colleagues at the Pentagon about what he actually did there either. In actual fact, he was an anomaly.

These thoughts had helped him believe that they would be shielded from the acid of accusation and innuendo that may come their way, because, in reality, they all knew exactly nothing. If he was ever to answer for his actions, he knew that all he had done was done in a careful and deliberate way, so that there was no one else to suffer for his actions except him and him alone, because only he knew what happened on 9/11, just as all the guilty ones did too.

Chapter 9

Transition Beach

The alarm on his bedside table made its usual presence known, just like it has done thousands of times before.

But this time, it really did sound different, not so urgent, then, the next sound he heard was the soft silken voice of Phillipa, his wife of twelve years and three kids gently asking, "How does it feel to be a civvy?" as she placed the tray with coffee and toast on his lap, before giving him a kiss.

As she did this he couldn't help but see the silhouette of her shapely and beautiful body of thirty- four years through her dressing gown.

The sunlight flooded the bedroom through the huge bay windows.

The holiday house was very close to the beach at Little Windy Bay, on Cat Island, in the Bahamas, a 'get away' gift from his folks after he was discharged from the Air Force some two weeks before.

"I don't know, but if it's going to be like this every day, great"! He laughed.

"Well, sweetheart, we are about to find out."

"Now that we have the next three months before you start at Honeywell, we are free of anything that will remind us of the last sixteen years, except for the love we have known all that time."

"And hopefully," she laughed, "to enjoy each other's company without any interruptions."

"Except I guess, when the kids crash through the door each morning when we get back."

"Be patient, my love. Just let me adjust to all this peace and quiet while we have it, because one thing I know is that it will be a strange experience for me to have everyone I will be working with at

Honeywell, milling around, asking a thousand questions a minute, at a million miles an hour, because at the Pentagon, no one said anything."

"They just did their jobs, heads down and bum up, no questions asked."

Phillipa then left the room to change for a day on the beach when his mind wandered back to the reality that seemed like light years away from here and thought that if everything he has planned went ass up, what would he really expect to happen?

From what he has seen happen to other whistle-blowers such as Bradley Manning and Daniel Ellsberg (patriots to him), he could be sure that the authorities would leave no stone unturned in their "search for the truth," completely destroying all in their path.

With the media as willing partners with their character assassination style of reporting, and their "to hell with the truth, just be first paper on the street" credo, it would be a blood bath, so.

He would have to be so careful in everything he did and said from now on, as he was not to know if every aspect of his life since his discharge was now being watched by the same agencies he once worked hand in hand with during his time of service to America.

After all, he did have access to the most secret secrets in the world and there would be lots of people out there who would have a vested interest in getting to know what he knows.

Right at the moment, and now that he had the chance, this time alone with Phillipa he hoped, would be the most beautiful and memorable time of their lives.

If he could, he was going to make it so, and being surrounded by the crystal clear waters of the most beautiful islands in the world with the palm trees growing right to the water's edge, the overall 'pleasure dome' atmosphere one gets here he thought was unbeatable.

On the beach, the sun seemed to drain him of every worry in the world as it penetrated every pore of his skin and, with his beautiful wife there rubbing suntan oil on his back, constantly reassuring him that their future was brighter than ever.

There could have been ten million people on the beach and he wouldn't have noticed a thing, being totally and blissfully unaware of everything.

That was, until he heard some men close by talking about what they had seen on CNN that morning, that the US government was now ready to put on trial in a military court the men who have been in custody at Guantanamo Bay for the last six years for planning the attacks on America on 9/11.

Chapter 10

"They misunderestimated me."
– George W. Bush

All the way home, Bevan was consumed with a silent rage, as he watched and heard what these so called leaders of our democracy were going to do to these innocent men from Guantanamo Bay. Just to keep the rage in the American public's chest from abating, these men, who had been blindfolded at the moment of their incarceration, flown to what they all thought was a possible execution in some dark room, then arriving at the bay to be relentlessly humiliated, demeaned, insulted, threatened, tortured, held in cages even dogs would be protected from being held in, their religious faith and traditions disrespected, all by boy soldiers who have never seen the face of war and, they themselves have been led to believe, that the whole Arab world deserves to be wiped from the face of the earth, all based on a racial and cultural hatred for them and people like them.

This way of thinking never sat well on Bevan's mind right from when all Americans were told to believe that these men were all involved in the planning of the attacks on America on 9/11.

To keep America informed, the glorious 'free press' we have in America was given 'limited' access to the Guantanamo facility, where they 'captured' some long-range photos of these people, the very first lot of 'detainees' who were bought to Guantanamo Bay.

They were in shackles, with blindfolds, shuffling to and fro in a bent-over stance, in the smallest of steps that the shackles allowed, being wheeled about on mortuary trolleys of plywood, in day-glow coveralls, all staged by our victorious military machine for the consumption of a justice-hungry America who were told that these evil men hated Americans, and they were all killers.

This was not the America he was raised to believe in, the one that always says that there really is liberty and justice for all, the America he willingly served faithfully for the last ten years, because after 9/11 when he joined up, he had noted with some concern the aggressive and resentful behaviour of his fellow servicemen to the information that they all heard on an almost hourly basis.

The 'propaganda' style of the government spin, done in such a way that if there was any doubt in anyone's mind, they were 'un-patriotic' and not worthy of what America has sacrificed for them.

"You are with us, or you are with the enemy."

"You choose, but when you do choose, grey is the only colour you are going to get from the US government as there is no more black or white any more, we will do your thinking for you, just keep the faith that we are doing the right thing for the whole world, you are safe now, we have everything under control."

In the meantime, there was a country that was being systematically being bombed and shot to death again by America, to make sure that democracy as Americans know it, will be their future way of life.

Yet strangely, what was being torn apart is the place where the culture of being a social species all began with what was a catastrophe for mankind.

America, you have done it again. God bless America. Ahmen.

Chapter 11

"All boy scouts should be prepared."
– Robert Baden-Powell

"Honey, I have been your constant companion for nearly half my life and I think I have got to know you pretty well, but the mood you have been in since we came back from the Bahamas is bewildering me.

Even the kids feel that something is going on, but you said I'm not to worry about it.

But how can I just ignore how different you have become in the last couple of weeks?

And the only thing I can think of is that you may be a little unsure of what you will doing and how you will fit in at Honeywell.

So please, tell me I could be close to the mark. I really want to help you with this transition and I am wondering if you really did become too dependent on the Air Force and the continuity it had."?

Bevan had closed down and had become almost incommunicado to nearly all who knew him.

Maybe, he thought, he just should trust the closest person to him.

His beautiful and constant friend, his wife. Yes!

She must know what I have done, he said quietly to himself, knowing it has to be done.

He really knew what it was that drove him constantly from behind, a pushing sensation he found hard to ignore.

There was an apprehension, the fear of the unknown that was wracking his brain.

What should be a straight-forward answer in his logical and methodical mind was not coming to his aid and it really pissed him off that this logical thinking and clear-thinking brain has had nothing to offer.

Well, not yet, anyway, but everyone was beginning to think that he was 'unwell,' especially his parents.

But it was a billion angry reasons that had him seething, making it really difficult to start the process of sensible action and direction, almost a form of paralysis, frozen to the spot.

He was like a blind man with a white cane in one hand and the other hand feeling its way along the wall, desperately looking for the beginning of the sidewalk that would be his way out of the alley.

But like all blind people, they can't make a move for fear of falling over or being run over if they step the wrong way.

What Bevan needed was something to help him take a step to anywhere at the moment.

Just one step to start moving, maybe like a seeing eye dog that could show him the way without words, just gentle nudges in the right direction, no pushing.

Three months and not a uniform in sight.

Wow, he thought, no more begging for time out.

It was not too hard to locate a nice house in the area of San Antonio to settle into as it was where he had spent the most of his growing and learning years before he joined the Air Force.

Being back in California now felt like he had never left. Phillipa had also made sure that the kids would be well cared for when it came to schools, sports, social and medical care and mixing with their friends again from years before, something they had made a point of maintaining from the moment they became a couple and moved away.

"Jay Rasmussen!? Shit, how did he get our number? Jesus, it's been years since I even thought of him because we all went to different colleges and did different things after we finished high school. But there is one thing I do remember about him.

It was when we were just kids at Junior High when we used to spend a lot of time down at the Newport pier fishing and watching all the senior high babes in their bikinis getting on the boats that used to go out to Katalina Island on summer break, and talking about when they would be old enough to do the same.

God, Phill, that was, like, so long ago!

"Did he leave a number at all or somewhere I could reach him, hun? On the freezer, huh?"

With some mixed feelings, Bevan called the number his wife had written on the freezer. As he held the receiver to his ear, he wondered how much his friend of so many years ago had changed, especially the sound of his voice.

"Jay! Hi, its Bevan Kleindinst. Yeah!, the very same, yeah!

It just blew me away to hear that you phoned, man!

And I am sorry I missed you as it was just the other day while I was having dinner with my wife that we were talking about all the kids we went to school and college with all those years ago.

Yeah? You too, huh? Well, before we get too far down that road, Jay, the reason I phoned and now that you have my number, I was hoping that you would like come over and snap a few beers with us here?

It just so happens that we are having some friends over for a barbeque tonight, so how about it?

Wanna' come over?

It would be great to see you again and maybe drift back a few years and crap on a bit, OK?

Sweet. Here is the address, Jay. It's 22b, Pamela Drive, Mountain View, Palo Alto, and as you are heading south, make a right into west El Camino Real off Grant Road, then as you go along Camino, look for Pamela on the left, maybe a block, ok? Cool.

See you then, Jay, bye!"

Bevan and Phillipa made everyone feel at home as they mingled with every one as they happily provided for everyone in a most sumptuous manner.

They hired a small, but highly recommended catering company from San Jose to do all the preparation and food for the whole event so that they could concentrate on their new and old friends completely, just as they always did when they lived in Virginia and had many high ranking officials from the Pentagon over for a dinner or a day on the porch having a barbeque.

But it all seemed to be over far too soon and it was like they only just arrived, then they were gone, all saying and waving their good byes to each other and making sure that they would all get together again real soon.

Even though there had been a lot of eating, drinking, and talking, it made Bevan wonder if it was something he did or didn't do?

The steaks were perfect as he recalled; well done and tender and the kids were well behaved. Everyone's mood was pleasant when they all sat down to some serious storytelling and banter by everyone who came, which actually started the minute they arrived, right up to the second they said their good byes.

Tonight was a welcome distraction from what had been on his mind, happily and eagerly engaging in conversations with everyone who was there and in an almost deliberate way, much like he used to do when living back in Virginia when he was a high-ranking officer in the Air Force where it was expected of him to be the social animal.

Tonight it was really different, like he really wanted to be involved, showing a genuine and keen interest in everything that they said and did, like he was screening them for reasons to NOT be part of their social circle. But it was one of the most enjoyable evenings with friends he had ever had.

Ever since they moved back to California from Virginia, Phillipa and Jay were gradually developing a group of friends who all seemed to enjoy each other's company.

Soccer mums and active in matters at the schools all their youngsters attend as they were all involved in the community, or had private practices and offices in San Jose and all lived close by and had kids in the same schools.

As they got ready to call it a night, Phillipa remarked to Bevan how much she enjoyed the evening and how nice it had been to see Jay fit in so well and that he seemed to be the one that most of the group seemed to zero in on during the evening.

Phillipa also said to Bevan that she was really pleased that Bevan and Jay were so comfortable with each other after all these years and that she noticed that it just so happened that the one person he spent more time with and showed more interest in was Jay, his boyhood friend.

Bevan agreed that it was a great night and that he found it really pleasant to go down memory lane with him and hear all he said in relation to his life so far, especially when they talked of their experiences in the military, a good solid base that many men have built a long-lasting and enduring friendship from, especially the fact that they had both been rapidly promoted through the ranks.

It was something that only happens because others noticed a quality in them and are willing to put a trust in their ability to get the job done. Yes, just like when he was a kid.

Before the evening began, Bevan and Jay had a small amount of time to renew their bonds before the others arrived.

Small talk in the beginning that was enlarged on by others who came as the evening unfolded.

"The Marines, huh?... And when were you discharged, bud?"

Were you in Baghdad?... Jeez ! How are you now?... Nah, I did the Air Force for a while, ten to be exact.

But I bailed out when my time was up to work at Honeywell again... Yeah, good all round on the package they offered and they seemed to be interested in some ideas I have, so I will see what it takes before I think of doing something on my own...but hey!"

This was the beginning of a conversation that went on all evening over some drinks, good food, and a stream of constant interruptions by others who also had stories to tell and an interest in what they were both talking about. Both of them were more than happy to be the centre of attention and occasionally, they both told entertaining stories that had humour with the odd sad one thrown in, just like two dogs sniffing around each other to see if there was anything to worry about, even though some of the stories seemed a little far-fetched, but never in anything they talked about to anyone who was there was a lie.

And when the evening came to its inevitable end, it was an evening that turned out to be better than what they had both ever imagined.

Mondays. Wow, how very different the traffic is here on the West Coast, thought Bevin as he drove into San Jose on his way to see his future employers but a little more excited today because he was about to be present at a meeting of all department heads of Honeywell Systems. They wanted to look at some of his programming ideas that they said they would possibly buy from him if what he had in mind fitted in with the new range of products they had developed and were getting ready to present to all three arms of the US military for their appraisal. He had worked with some of the tech staff at the Pentagon some years before, so he felt quite comfortable about what was to take place today.

He remembered what Jay was telling him at the barbeque about his time in the Marines as a communications analyst specialist when he was in Iraq and all the coms traffic they had to move around that would assist the drone homes (drone airfields) plan their targets for the day and what it involved and how he thought it could be improved but no one would take him seriously.

Bevan was actually wondering if Jay would be interested in being involved in some way with the creation of some new programming ideas (a knowing smile drifted across Bevan's face).

Bevan listened intently as Jay started talking about his Purple Heart. As it turned out, Jay had been in command of an acoustic decipher company, a unit whose sole task was to piece together all the generated verbal data information from the radio comms they were scanning that was passing between the groups of insurgents in their area, all while getting a fix on where these radios were to pinpoint their position and predict where these enemy tanks could be possibly intercepted with drone-launched munitions, hopefully well before they could do any damage.

This was all bought together by the Decipher Jockeys (DJs) as they were called, who would constantly download the latest satellite and drone images of their area of responsibility, load them into a computer that would look for and highlight any changes in the imagery it found and it would then compare it with all the other stored images downloaded the day before.

Then the final image in digital form was then sent to the dronehome so that the mission planners there could set up a field of interest in the drone's mission computer by loading the final image into its flight plan along with the "pings" (the last pinpointed radio fix) and as it was flying over these areas, where the on-board cameras searched for actual differences within the areas highlighted on the mission map.

When it saw something, it was then compared with what was in the ping pak, and would then target it for a strike.

If the optics reader on board saw any difference between the real-time images coming through the camera compared to the on-board digital image and what the ping pak saw, then the pilot in Virginia USA would call for a strike.

And subject to confirmation, if the ground teams were seeing the same:

Boom!

Chapter 12

Good Move

The best-laid plans of men and mice always go awry. Don't count your chickens before they hatch.

Fools rush to where angels fear to tread.

He had heard these sayings from all kinds of people in all kinds of situations all his life, but today, they seemed to have more relevance than at any other time.

The Honeywell management had made their intentions very clear as to what they wanted Bevan to be involved in when it came to the development and research of new processing technology and the programmes to run them. Bevan would also become their spokesman to the interested parties from the DOD as, in their view, he "spoke their language."

Remembering the Wikileaks release in 2010 of the embassy cables' information and the "gun cam" images from the Apache attack helicopter in Basra by PFC Bradley Manning from his base in Kabul, Afghanistan, Bevan quietly came to the big decision to start making preparations for the telling of his story to Jay.

Bevan's thoughts were of a best of time and the good memories of days gone bye that helped us come to terms with things that are thrust upon us in this ever-changing world, a time that is full of new circumstances, almost on an hourly basis.

Bevan was well pleased with the impression left in people's heads after meeting Jay. In particular, how he seems to have adjusted to being out of the rigid routine the Marines imposed on its members quite well.

Renewing their friendship after almost fifteen years seemed to be a good move.

Their high school years had been intense, especially trying to plan a future around the events of the days of the 90's.

In hindsight, though, some of their best interactions happened when they were in college, ripe with the possibilities of real prospects and the continuous stream of intensely pushy women, looking for a secure end to their insecurity and a new beginning.

He had chosen to leave it to the last minute to make the move, but he was totally unaware of fact that it really is about to change history.

With all this in mind, he had to face up to the decision he had made in releasing the information he had saved in relation to the truth of what happened on the day the Pentagon got involved in the direct actions of 9/11.

But if it is to be a total commitment, he must tell his wife of his situation, having to make a decision on how, when, where, and why he has to reveal the hard facts discovered to the world and, what an impact, good or bad, it will have, all depends on whether he has their total support.

Bevan believes he has a fair idea of how their thinking is guided, having all a deep sense of being 'American.' Something special!

One of the many "concerns" Bevin was dealing with was the direct impact on him first and whether anyone would employ him after disclosing 'secrets.'

Be they government, military or domestic commerce, being a recipient of an award from the early Silicon Valley gooks for being the creator of a program for a system that stores and can cross-match DNA profiles of millions of registered DNA sequences in milliseconds with a hundred percent accuracy rescan sequence that looks for mismatch possibilities to eliminate any doubt in the data on file.

Something he was proud of and it cemented his place in the folk law of those who had come and gone in such a short amount of time and created such legacies along the way. (Blame it all on the dot com era and their greed to profit from people's ignorance of the digital storm.)

Now is the time to be as logical as he has ever been, he thought, under the circumstances, knowing that if he left it too long, the anticipated impact he hopes will eventually may be a lost opportunity to right a terrible wrong he believes he has discovered.

In all reality, the up-bringing he experienced really prevented any other choice but to go ahead, or, forever suffer the guilt and self-inflicted wounds of his own mind for failing to do so.

The freedom in the work he is doing for others since his discharge has been a welcome distraction from the gnawing of his teeth when his mind inevitably strays back to the imaginings of scenarios and outcomes of what he is committed to reveal.

The one thing that he will not let happen is that he will not end up in the gutter for being accused of treason for choosing only the worst that happened at the Pentagon that fits the conspiracy gook network.

But overall, Bevan was comfortable and in control. There were no alarm bells going off in his head, as he looked to be taking everything in his stride, not ever, letting minor irritants manifest and spoil the sense of impending well-being he has been feeling that is on the increase.

Bevan has always managed to find just the right words at the right time when diplomacy is the key for, and every time he has had something on his mind, that he knows his wife will listen intently and offer a wise word without being judgemental about the subject raised for comment.

Or at least, he knows he has her trust and support.

He could only say to Phillipa what he had in his possession and how he came to be the owner, in very few words, leaving the anger and resentment out of the talk that he personally has felt ever since he realized what he had been witness to, while simply doing what he was employed to do.

He offered no 'reason' or 'explanation' to Phillipa.

As he had no guilt or shame for obtaining what he has and in no way, was he trying to make an attempt to justify or endorse his motives to her because of what she may have been thinking herself.

Except to say that this is where it gets blurred, that being the pronounced difference between good and bad or right he feels and wrong and how high he had set his standards and if he still believes what all that red white and blue flag waving stuff means every fourth of July, and all that Bevan wants when being judged is to be found right smack in the middle, where the "feeling good to be an American" can be felt, all the way down to the bottom of your snake skin boots.

Is it great to be an American when so many places that looked to America as a giant big brother ended up being thoroughly polluted with "Americana." All in the name of 'freedom' or 'democracy.'

Words big and intimidating, making sure we must have these ideals as the things to rule the world with, using them as their protective shields.

Leaving no room for any other group-style thinking and dissenting factions, after all the doors to those liberties we take for granted are now closed for general consumption.

These and many other conversations he had with himself over the last twelve months. Working out just how bad he would feel if he did nothing at all, and the possible and in some ways inevitable pointing fingers if it all goes butt up.

I should write a book, he thought, like many others who had something about the events of 9/11 onbtheir minds.

But doing a book would only let the information out in "dribs and drabs." It should be an 'in your face' statement backed up with the CCTV footage he has.

Who to fear and who to trust with this vital information is truly the linchpin.

Gathering credible and authoritative people around him, like a defensive shield in his obligation to reveal the most vivid discussions to take place among highest ranking public servants in charge of defence, home security, and all armed services, all being appointed by the Commander in Chief to bring America to where it is today—anarchy!

The secretaries of all the armed services wings talking candidly about the deceit of the events on that day and what will they do now that an inner government, made up of all the most highly appointed men and women with a common goal in mind have planned what to do. 'If all else fails,' the President really could be terminated.

But on Bevan's mind, there is much more to this than just a conversation recorded of those who had every right to feel secure and safe in the way they all became involved in this fabrication of a 'safety net' scenario, planned well ahead of the final events, and all thinking their trail should not be traced, thinking, they had control "rights" as an appointed official over every aspect of data collection and storage.

Based on who they were, in the pecking order of the day.

More reasons Bevan has pondered, in the days, weeks and months after 911, why no one actually made any inquiries about the camera data that happened on that day.

As everywhere you care to look inside the Pentagon building complex, cameras in all shapes and sizes are gulping down all of the feeding frenzy we do on a daily basis there, to become so used to them being all around us that we actually don't 'see' them anymore.

This is possibly why these heavy hitter from all different backgrounds came here to grind out who will be a new threat from some far off land, to our democracy and possibly, some of us at home.

Chapter 13

Why Integrity is
Worth the Consequences

Jay asked Bevan one question after Bevan had told him of what he had from the Pentagon.

"When do you want this put in the right hands?"

Surprised by the question, Bevan stared at his friend in a state of overwhelming joy and shock.

Thinking that he must make it better understood, what he had that would stop the rot of all this government activity to keep the false story they had been telling the American public since 9/11 happened on track.

Wondering if Jay had fully grasped the gravity of what Bevan had explained in his reach out to his long-time friend about something that will either continue to change what has happened to change America completely, such as the 20-year war that followed from the 'attack' from the Middle East on 9/11 did, he asked Jay again.

"You do understand what I am saying here, Jay?"

A pretext to war was always on their minds.

Planning, years ahead, a scenario of events before the 'attack' was made.

The 'first' time the WTC became a target of terrorists with an agenda was 27 February 1993 at 3:17 AMAEST.

The second time the WTC became the target of terrorists was 11 September 2001 at 9:03 AM.

Now having every reason to declare it a "Second Pearl Harbor" and all its connotations.

This is how these few could go about establishing an American military presence in the Middle East without raising suspicions became the goal of the day.

But there will be those who still believe that it was only to shore up the supplies of oil that America presented a plan to 'liberate' Kuwait by the Senior Bush administration.

Some, who still have some doubt about the politics involved, were left wringing their hands in anguish at the thought of even worse to come if we don't get it now.

Watching, seeing how the wholesale move of the American armed forces to the Middle East happened in one fell swoop—it just might be the best con job ever pulled on the world by the Bush administration.

As what will get the attention of Hussein and Khomeini of Iran to believe America meant what it said it would do if they didn't toe the line and get out of Kuwait?

To come up with an overwhelming show of military might that would make those who wished, at any time, there was an option, to extend the "conflict" would be subject to a thorough beating for the Arabs at the hands of the much better trained and equipped US army.

All the American diplomats were selling the idea of American protection for them while Saddam Hussein was being the master of ceremonies, and it was not a hard thing to do, as most of the residents were being terrified by the one man feared by all other Arabs who had a different path to Mecca mapped out than Hussein.

Having persuaded all the Arab countries that surrounded Kuwait that to set up a base that would have everything it needed to conduct a long-term war against anyone who would challenge any of the American allies would guarantee their defence by all the coalition hardware shipped into the area.

Instigated and orchestrated by those members of the US shadow government, to fly in all that was required to make the presence of America a direct challenge to those who had other plans for the world's oil supplies.

All these men of the shadow government were all Presidential appointees.

All who planned that at the end of their days of "representing the American people" stood to make a handsome profit from their time 'in Service of the American people.'

Such is the 'American way' when it comes to a life involved in politics.

There has always existed those who have faced the question and the resolution to a fact that sometimes, men get too ambitious and start doing things to alter the balance of that that was the victor that on the fourth of July 1776 these men created on the same day, a 'shadow government' , watching the performance of all and sundry within the halls of power this great nation became the United States of America.

Men who have had discussions of "what if it all fails?"

As a matter of common sense and social obligation. (Some will have a differing opinion.)

As people will only do the bidding of those they can put their trust in to make sure men and all mankind will never have to question anyone's intentions about who they are representing and what they value.

These discussions, mostly held in private, all centred around what they think will be the better alternative to a failing or failed system of government that could happen at any time.

Something no doubt that led to the issue being mentioned in the Declaration of Independence and the Constitution.

Something that some Americans had taken to heart was that all Americans must follow and accept this change wholeheartedly or be an enemy of the state.

As George Bush Junior was once quoted as saying: "You are with us or you're with them."

In truth, a move forcing Americans to 'choose sides,' giving the Bush admin sweeping powers likened to a refined dictatorship modelled on the WWII German design and those who had shown how to suppress the masses and how to change society to a herd mentality.

That was called 'The Patriot Act'

Acceptance of what we were told, it seemed, was a necessary evil if democracy is to be the victor.

It was Bush Senior, H.W. Bush being the first to grasp at something that helped perpetuate the resentment towards those who had been swiftly blamed by America's political elite for the events of that day on 9/11, appealing to the American public on TV for the permission to step into the events taking place following the Iraqi military entering Kuwait with the intention of bringing Kuwait to her knees, according to the story told by the daughter of the Kuwait ambassador to America.

"That Iraqi troops were seen stealing humidicribs from the women's hospital in Kuwait and throwing these babies that were once in them on the tiled floor to die."

It was from this story where GH Bush was front and centre, played out on the floor of the US Congress and on national television, by this girl who was nowhere near the event she was portraying, all to enrage those who were all ready wanting blood for the twin towers.

And that an overwhelming presence of the Iraqi armed forces were in Kuwait to terminate any more oil leaving the Middle East that could finance Kuwait.

It was the speech by HW Bush Senior that persuaded the American public and the world that what had happened on 9/11 was something the whole world had to be involved in and as soon as possible, put a stop to this "invasion" by Iraq if the world was to be free again.

America was 'under attack', not by any known or recognised military power, but 'terrorists in the mountains of Afganastan' who had thought out and implemented the most complex plan to destroy America from within it's own borders.

This is where it was soon to be shown just what corruption makes those who are always looking for some personal advantage to be gained by the fact they are now members of one of the most sought after military powers in existence today.

Corruption or 'the greasy palm.'

All this aside, Bevan had made the first move. No second chance.

All this information, just at a time there seemed to be a movement becoming established who transmitted their intentions to "clear away the fog" when, we are all, at some time, addressing matters that directly affects the everyday existence we all took for granted.

"Their support could prove invaluable, being on the lookout for deals done under tables to prove their claims and integrity".

Something that gave Bevan the reassurance that what will be done will not be disregarded out of hand but will get a fair hearing.

But when it comes to offering up the goods on the 'establishment' to these people and the operators within, it will have to be presented in such a way as to immediately exonerate Bevan and his 'friends' from any charge of treason or an activity that would harm America in any way, all due to the integrity of the data retrieved and what it says.

All on time-stamped visuals with copies made for security requirements of the day. (A Congressional Library requirement when digital is part of the system with high security.)

But for some, who may be put under scrutiny when applying their relative values to questions of strength of heart in remaining flexible but resolute in using the words we chose to carry our favour and opinion, there was a sense of no blame and none accused. It's just inevitable 'change' happening.

There is this need emerging in this generation's society for us to start trusting again.

To restore the once "true values" we were all encouraged to pursue as life went on, as the pinnacle of all why we care and show compassion for each other.

That now, for some strange reason, those "values" and what that means don't seem to hold the same 'value' of those values our folks first established.

(Sort that one out, he thought.)

Jay was talking to his constant companion, a German short-haired pointer with an eagerness to lick you all over for a pat and a scratch from you on any occasion.

A 'blog ' he thought seems to be the only and possibly, best way to 'get it out there' type of urgency.

"Internet surfing on steroids." (Is there such a thing as "Blog bog?") (Nothing to think of or take to task the twits of this world loose on the communication revolution network.

But Jay is already fully aware that being 'out there' is no guarantee that it can offer him a true barrier between those who will think you need investigating and then, those who follow the doctrine of the unplugging of the end of your power cord, shutting you down completely.

(Thinking some more).

"How about direct everyday television news and cable with a hunger for being the 'first to bring you breaking NEWS." ?

Is this where he thinks Bevan will feel and be safe?

Out in the bright lights for all to see and "clear of the fog?"

No hiding behind a smoke screen like a coward.

Like anyone pondering a life change, not of his making, the fear of the unknown can be crippling.

Jay was not immune from these emotions, even though he had the knack for smoothing ruffled feathers around others he knows, making them feel better.

A natural 'carer,' he still had to, like it, not ruffle someone's feathers if he was to live with himself.

He wonders if he is only feeling strange because of the relentless feeling of something tugging at you, drawing your attention to the possible effect these revelations will have on one and all after the big picture is laid out for all to see and make their own minds up about what they will see.

"That's the way I was taught to think. Like a patriotic citizen."

He could also become the centre of the attacks by those who think he had other alternatives, whatever they will be on their minds, as they discredit him and all those associated with him in this disclosure.

Jay wonders what it could be like, just how willing would those Americans be, to really answer the call of "truth and retribution?"

Who become overpowered with the urgency in their chests to respond in a way that is filled with a damn good reason to be part of the change.

And the right side of history.

Those who are now 'woke' are rightfully forcing the point that this type of expository journalism is still as vitally important as it always has been if we are going to get what we expect of them.

"Keeping the bastards honest" should be constantly demanded that their politicians who they elected will be serving the people only.

All of us, bar none, base our future on a sense of right and wrong, mostly developed by people who are governed by that thinking.

That, with their generous financial gift, they may have made a difference in one of the looted people's lives we have left behind, those victims of the West's 'intervention' to clean up what was seen as unhealthy for US interests.

Those who, on other's instructions, lost it all and got nothing back from those who said, "But we did it in your own best interests."

But those with self-interests at home will say that we all should be outraged at others first, to let us off the hook, of not being humane to our own, too, especially if we are all then expected to turn a blind eye to all the examples of how callous we humans can be to each other not only at home, but elsewhere in the world.

But then, on the home front, are they to be expected to calmly respond in an unemotional manner when they find out that their own government is the enemy?

Or, do they carry on like nothing has changed. ?

Given the media's abuse of the truth, all we will see is the media, make some other wild grab for a better feeling story that will be used as an example for behaving the way they do, to this, or any other crisis portrayed as something other than what it really was.

Mainly so that it becomes more acceptable the longer it goes on, especially by those who have had a change of heart after their bank accounts were the recipients of many 'Thank you's' that helped persuade their sense of fairness.

And it's not hard to imagine all these captains of industry, in the back rooms of management meetings.

A 'chat between friends,' as they discuss the possibility of seizing power one day, like what the Nazis and the dictators of Europe did during WWII.

All through legal channels, of course, and without firing a shot, except in self-defence.

So many radical events where we see now that we all seem to be becoming complacent and indifferent about life's events. "As it has had no real effect on me, why should I care?"

Except that there is always the unlucky few who were sadly made into another notch in the handle of a gun that is, thousands of years old. Ho hum.

Chapter 14

"Hi, and welcome to the Republic."

After all the time the 'cloak and dagger' theatrics rampaged, mostly only through his mind and then, seeing with his own eyes, what he had done, and it filled him with an overpowering feeling of dread.

The immediacy of the response to his disclosure was not expected, as every news outlet in the country, then the world, made it 'viral.'

Let alone the prolific and immediate solutions and suggestions on offer by those who had sat at home for an hour to digest the information they saw that makes it look that the USA government of the day had a direct hand in the flying of numerous aircraft around the sky, only to have them intentionally impact two of the most iconic buildings on American soil that represented a nation's ambitions and wealth.

And a war is what we were told we needed, to get that "feeling" back again. The thing that would purify America and give her back her soul.

Turning out, at that point in time, to be 10 years of it.

Nothing said in an honest word that would allay all the fears of the impending revolution that is about to set fire to the American way of life, an American government, and the changes due to happen for the benefit of all mankind.

Not just those in the cities of America, but around the world.

Most are fully unaware that at the rate of the consumption of our finite resources, how we have devoured at an alarming rate in the last 300 years resources that could have lasted a millennium, we would be bitten in the ass by the dire consequences.

If we don't stop devouring this planet every day, perhaps we only have a hundred years left.

The media exposure had to happen, but with the media the way it is now, they will make sure it will be talked about by the whole world in no time flat.

Maybe, this just might change how our democracy works, under the former interpretation and what it actually means.

The interview.

Bevan and his support team had thought through every angle as to why he had chosen to reveal what he had in such a way, was, to protect him from all negative publicity from those who would want to cast aspersions and impune his credibility.

As to go to the 'authorities', being the FBI or CIA made him sceptical, knowing that on the tapes were members of both organizations verbally involved in the discussions relating to the planning of the passengers 'disappearance'.

The roll-on effect.

Now that everything Bevan Kleindinst had to tell the American people about what really happened on 911 been revealed, it took on a life of it's own.

The main stream news media outlets, in their bid to publish more sensational writings than all others, there was an endless stream of media stories on all international and national news outlets, both on line and in all the social media platform's, that presented the strongest argument for demanding that all governments, be they domestic, federal or international, to start behaving in such a way that the people who elected them could once again trust them them to be as open and honest as they once were, especially in the way they conducted business 'In the best interests of those who want a decent life' to once again, feel safe in everything they do every day.

The main thrust of their oped's was the true meaning of what a democracy is and what it is supposed give those who live under the promis it offers everyone, and how the failure to keep all those people who make up our governing bodies accountable in every aspect of that power that no one could argue against, except at their loss of their integrety and trust that will now take years for all people in all walks of life to recover from.

Those detained.

For all those who were identified on the CCTV imagry as being involved in the planning and the carrying out of this attack on America, the law men were not far behind with the detainment of all those revealed in the disclosure that followed were to become a shock to the whole world, of just how far out of control they became, in their quest to see America become the dominant power player of what was to be, the new world order.

If only, in their own imaginations, they believed that what they had done for years was in the best interest of all world citizens, no matter what or who paid the ultimate price, and that they would never be held responsible, believing in their own importance.

The End.

www.ingramcontent.com/pod-product-compliance
Lightning Source LLC
Chambersburg PA
CBHW070447170726
48291CB00005B/1641